THE GHOSTS OF CHARUMA FOREST

AND OTHER STORIES

SOTER LUCIO

STRATTON
—PRESS—
Publishing Life

Stratton Press Publishing
831 N Tatnall Street Suite M #188,
Wilmington, DE 19801
www.stratton-press.com
1-888-323-7009

ISBN (Paperback): 978-1-64895-125-1
ISBN (Ebook): 978-1-64895-126-8

Printed in the United States of America

CONTENTS

ACKNOWLEDGMENTS

T hanks to my daughter, Teresina, for her unwavering patience in helping bring this work to fruition.

THE GHOSTS OF
CHARUMA FOREST

C lyde sauntered through the blinding rain in the dead of night and cautiously navigated the dangerous curves from memory. Once per year, he'd religiously set out on that perilous trek to visit his grandparents. Not only was the path strewn with treacherous roots threatening to trap the feet of those walking along, but there was the ever-present ghost and soucouyant lurking in the shadows. That meant double trouble for the unwary and the stranger who choose to hike without a guide.

Christmas was special for old folks, and being the first grandson, he had a duty to perform. The ghosts of Charuma Forest were quiet on this particular night, but Clyde wouldn't let that fool him. He had in his possession the three sticks of matches, some grains of garlic, and the special prayers that were handed down throughout the generations. Although his formative years were spent in the capital city of Port of Spain, his parents ensured that he knew his heritage.

He had the tools for his protection and defense safely tucked away and easily accessible in the front pocket of his trousers, specifically made for this occasion, this terrain, and this atmosphere.

The trunk with his belongings would follow on donkey cart in the next few days. He was of the seventh generation of the strong and ancient family from the Charuma Forest situated in the northern range of the island.

He couldn't help but think of the stories of his great-grandmother who'd hung herself from the silk cotton tree after the birth of her second baby. It is said that she espied her husband in the forest with one of the maids in a compromising position. That hurt her so deeply, that after a period of depression, she left the house dressed in her favorite gown, reserved for Christmas Eve night mass at the cathedral in the city, and never returned. Though they searched for her over a lengthy period, she was not found till after six months.

Subsequent to that horrid but sad affair, the maids complained of a mournful cry in the woods on their way home on afternoons. That escalated to cries in the main house, but was heard only by the maids.

They were told that the house was quite old, built before the island was discovered by Christopher Columbus, and there was bound to be some noises as is the case with old buildings. The framework was hardwood, which expands and contracts according to the weather. The maids did not ask for an explanation for the crying in the forest. They needed their jobs.

Clyde's great-grandfather was a consummate lecher and degenerate. His lasciviousness was known far and wide, and the parents would threaten their children, including their sons, with disinheritance should they ever be found to have any contact with him. It wouldn't have been surprising to learn that he'd seduced some underage girl and impregnated her to the ruin of herself and family because he was an extremely handsome and charming man. But his great-grandmother threatened to do away with herself if she couldn't marry the man with whom she was so desperately in love. Her parents, with a heavy heart, gave in to her demands, something they regretted for the rest of their lives, which was spent in deep sorrow and dismay at their inability to save their only child from the constant heartaches and deep resentment meted out to her by her husband.

Clyde was so engrossed in remembering the story that he was oblivious to his surroundings and didn't realize that he made a wrong turn until he was right smack in the clearing where stood the ill-fated silk cotton tree. He was aghast with a devastating fright that descended upon him so suddenly that he scrambled away from that accursed area, but did not envisage going deeper and deeper into the menacing forest where the more aggressive ghosts did exist, unable to cross the sacred boundaries planted by the seer of long, long ago. He only realized where he was when the pungent, malodorous, and acrid scent burnt his nostrils and the trees scratched when he touched them.

He was in uncharted territory, since they were forbidden from crossing a certain demarcation from time immemorial. He stood there wondering which way to turn while trying to recognize the various scents and also from which direction, when he heard the sound of an animal, specifically a lion.

He turned in the direction of the sound but didn't see anything, not even a movement from the branches. Then there was another indefinable sound behind him. Again he turned and saw nothing. Different sounds kept coming at him from behind, and he spent his time spinning and searching for the source of the strange sounds until he was dizzy and couldn't make out from which direction he had come.

Sure now that it was a Lougahoo, he retrieved the matches from his pocket and in quick succession, lit three of them as instructed. The strange sounds immediately stopped, but he knew that wouldn't be for long.

He took to his heels and ran. He just ran. He didn't care where, but run he did, because it could only be away from.

Eventually, he came to another clearing and surmised that he was on safe territory. He stopped to catch his breath, and that's when the inhuman laughter pierced his hearing. It quickly progressed into a spine-chilling growl so terrifying that Clyde stood transfixed, unable to move. His body had had enough of scares and so went into something akin to shock. He felt himself falling as in slow motion and hit his head hard on the root of a tree. He saw stars but didn't question whether they were in the sky or simply as a result of the lash from dropping on the root.

When he came to, the sun was overhead, so he reckoned that he was out for a good many hours. Although he still didn't know where he was, he heard the sound of water flowing and followed the sound till he found the river. He followed it downstream and eventually got to his grandmother's house by sundown.

His grandmother found him at the gate and brought him into the house.

"Don't tell me you passed through the dark forest. How did you end up there?"

"Granny, I got lost. Marie was on my mind, and I couldn't stop thinking about her."

"My mother? Oh Yes. She does that at this time of the year. Didn't your mother tell you to keep a grain of garlic in your mouth?"

"If she did, I don't remember it. What's that supposed to do?"

"Keeps the ghosts of Charuma Forest from taking hold of your mind. She's powerful at Christmas time. And the other ghosts follow suit. In the past few years, she's been getting pretty awful. Like she's out for revenge. She now hurts where she never used to. She used to cry only. But now…"

"We're all in trouble?"

"The maids have all left without notice—that is, all but one. Miranda is still here because she's got nowhere to go. Of course we're grateful for that. Not nice, but there it is. We need each other. And she is quite capable in spite of her age. She can navigate this old house where no one else can."

"She must be quite old now. How can she manage this house?"

"Oh, she no longer has duties to perform like the old days. She does as she pleases. Whatever and whenever she chooses to. Of course, we hope she never chooses to stop cooking."

"Oh yes, I remember her cooking all too well," Clyde remarked as he rubbed his belly and licked his lips.

"I think some of the story got lost with the passage of time and a bit of life in the city. Come with me. You can freshen up later. First things first," she told him.

Clyde followed her down the long winding hallway and then down some steps, where he was handed a lamp.

"I don't remember this part of the house. Was it off limits?" Clyde asked with a shiver as he walked through the narrow hallway. He wondered why the temperature of this part of the house was way lower than the rest but didn't voice his musings.

"Something like that. Soon you shall see why. Come on."

She unlocked the heavy oak door, and when they entered, he was struck by the richness of the furnishings. It was quite unlike the rest of the house, and he again wondered why this was so. His grandmother then told him the story.

"In the old days, there were a lot of warring between the residents. Everyone wanted all the land, not just a few acres for themselves. So they all used their knowledge of the dark arts to ensure no one else got land. All the gold that you see here was the price paid for said land. They cannot be used as a bargaining chip for anything else because they don't belong to us. They are the property of the spirits in return for the defense of the land."

Clyde, with a frown, asked for clarification.

"Well, it's like this. The old ones recited some incantations in a strange language and summoned a vicious but well-focused entity and requested him to obtain for them the land that they wanted. That done, they had to put aside some gold, which in those days were quite plentiful, and they were never to use it for any reason whatsoever."

"Now I understand. Are all these papers related to the spirits also?"

"I was just getting to those. Some are about the ghosts in the forbidden part of the forest. But there is one that explains the life and death of my mother, who now haunts and jeopardizes the lives of the maids. She's grown quite vengeful over the past few years. That also has something to do with the ghosts that were paid for a service. My mother is considered a squatter. She's got no right inhabiting the domain of the original spirits."

"What!" Clyde exclaimed, mouth hanging open. "A ghost squatting? You're joking right? You can't be serious."

"Oh yes. I assure you, I'm quite serious. You see, my mother was once a human being and upon committing suicide, was unable to move on, so she's now a ghost haunting the area where she died. The original ghosts of the Charuma Forest never had human form. I think they're called entities."

"So in the forest, we have a group of entities, plus Marie's ghost?"

"Yes."

"The ghosts can't cross a certain line, but Marie can. Am I right?"

"Correct."

"That's the reason it is now so dangerous. They are fighting for turf!" Clyde felt like he'd gotten to the crux of the matter. "Oh well, I would really like to know something about Marie. All the information I have is that she was quite beautiful. Just that. I've never heard of a description." Since his grandmother just raised her eyebrow without uttering a word, he continued, "Was she tall, dark, straight hair, curly hair? Did the sound of her laughter make all and sundry forget their troubles for a while? I do want to know about her when she was alive. You were the baby when she died?"

To Clyde, knowing something more of this particular ancestor took precedent over the stories about ghosts haunting maids. It's highly unlikely that he'd ever be a maid. Right?

"Well, if you'd hold on a bit, we'd get to that. As to your last question, yes, I was the baby. I never knew her. But I was always told about her, so I felt like I did. My father, however, was a different kettle of fish. I was told very little, and what I did know was garnered from bits and pieces overheard through closed doors and cracks in the walls."

"Sorry, Grandma."

"Nothing to be sorry about. Well, from what I've gathered, she was average height, dark, straight nose, eyes that slant upward, with thick bushy eyebrows, high cheekbones, and a ready smile for everyone. Her waist-length hair was kind of frizzly. Not curly, more like the frizzle fowl. But as far as I understand, quite beautiful. And she carried it quite well."

A strong wind suddenly came in, from where they don't know, and all the gold pieces tumbled from their perches. Amid the clatter, Granny distinctly heard someone saying, "Get him out of my house." She held on to the nearest post for support, and with bulging eyes and fear for her life, she gawked at Clyde.

"What is it Granny?" he asked.

"Didn't you hear that voice?" Her voice trembling.

"What voice? I didn't hear anything. Just all the gold knocking each other. Must have been an earthquake."

She grabbed his arm and pulling him along, said, "Come on. Let's get out of here. She hustled him out, all the while not saying a word and Clyde complaining that he doesn't understand the rush.

"We can't run from an earthquake, Granny," he volunteered.

"That wasn't an earthquake, sonny-boy. Hurry."

Meeting Miranda on the way out, they stopped and stared at the expression of horror on her face. She stifled a scream by covering her mouth with her hand, turned, and practically ran away as fast as her arthritic legs could carry her. Going in to the first room, she slammed the door and turned the key.

"Granny? What was that all about?"

"I have no idea," she answered, puzzled.

"She look like she's seen a ghost. And a terrible one at that."

"Maybe she did. Let's keep going. On second thought, you go on. I'll go check on her. Do you remember the way to your room?"

"Yes."

"Good. You go freshen up. I'll come get you after."

Granny duly went and knocked on the door. She had to say she was alone before Miranda would open the door.

"Who was that man, Miss Rosetta?" she asked as soon as the door was locked again, trembling like a leaf.

"My grandson Clyde. Don't you remember him?" Granny watched her closely, head tilted to the side in extreme puzzlement. Miranda does have a sharp memory. What could be the matter?

"Oh no. That's not Clyde. That's your father."

"Don't be ridiculous, Miranda. Do you feel all right? Here. Come sit. I know you've been doing too much." Miranda vehemently shook away the proffered hand and in a voice Rosetta never heard before, said between gritted teeth, "Don't patronize me."

Rosetta stared, dumbfounded. "What do you mean, Miranda? That boy can't possibly be my father.

"Oh yes, he can. And he is."

"But that's impossible!" Rosetta, trying to figure out what's going on with Miranda, paced the floor, hands clasped on her chest.

"Come here. You sit. Do you remember your childhood? How everyone always spoke to you about your mother?" Miranda made a swift recovery so as not to further cause Rosetta any more upsets with her shocking revelations.

"Yes."

"But never your father?"

"Yes. I don't have a memory of a single word about him. No."

"There was a reason for that. He wasn't just bad, Rosie."

"What was he?" Rosetta, sitting at the edge of her seat, felt her heart pounding in anticipation of what words were coming next.

"He was an evil man, so evil that one day, I saw him spit on the grass outside, and a few hours later, the grass was all burnt."

"That could have been coincidence. Up here, it's quite hot in the dry season. Especially in the middle of it. Like April and May. The entire mountain would be dry. Not a green leaf could be seen."

"Not dry, Rosie. Burnt."

"I don't understand. What exactly do you mean?"

"It was like he spit acid that literally burnt the grass. I did tell one of the elders in the village about it. I was told to stay very far from him because it shows the nature of the man."

"Now I understand the saying, 'Be careful what you let out of your mouth.'"

"Where on earth did you hear that?"

"Through a hole in a wall," she answered, unashamed.

"Eavesdropping. You naughty thing," said Miranda, playfully shaking an accusing finger at her.

"Yes. So what's all this have to do with what's going on now?"

"The ghosts of Charuma Forest have been acting up for a few weeks now. The possibility exist that they knew your father was coming."

"Stop saying that. He's my grandson. He is Clyde."

"And I say he is not. Garrison had enough knowledge to return after death and remember himself. This way, he can exact revenge on the family and collect all the gold, for which reason he did marry your mother."

14

"Utter nonsense. You can't control what happens after death. Including your own."

"Do you know where he is now? And what he's doing?" asked Miranda.

"No. Do you?" Rosetta answered.

"No. You should go see," Miranda said in a voice that could be considered commanding.

"I will." Rosetta got up to leave, but turned around, forefinger tapping her chin. "Wait. Before I go, if he had so much of that kind of knowledge, why didn't he just take it before dying back then?"

"Your grandmother also had some knowledge. Remember the owners of the gold? She'd made a new agreement with them. Don't ask me the details. I don't have that kind of knowledge. But I think you do."

"What on earth do you mean by that?"

"Go check on the boy. I'll tell you when you get back." She pushed her gently between the shoulder blades. Rosetta walked away but a bit puzzled, she repeatedly turned to look over her shoulder. Miranda had moved on to other things because she opened drawers and gathered a few items like oils and powders in little vials.

Meanwhile, Rosetta got to the end of the corridor and heard a muffled sound from within the last bedroom. Pressing her ear to the door, she distinctly heard the words "too soon." She recognized the voice as one of the older, most trusted maids. She left before she could be discovered. Moving along to the room where Clyde should have been, she found the door opened but no sign of Clyde. Hearing footsteps from behind, she turned, and there was Clyde rummaging in a bag. Not seeing her, he let out some curse words and a big fat steups, like what the older folks from the village would use when confronted with an insurmountable problem.

"Such language! Tut-tut! Is that what city life has taught you? Not nice."

"I'm sorry, Granny. Didn't see you there. You know I have total respect for you. I would never use such words in your presence."

"Don't worry about it. Enjoy your youth. It is short enough."

"Were you looking for me?"

15

"Yes. Are you ready to eat?"

"Granny, I'm famished. Miranda's cooking for dinner?"

"Naturally. Let's go. Did you find everything to your liking?"

"Huh?"

"Your room?"

"Oh yes. Yes. All's good."

Entering the dining room, they met with one-hundred-ninety-pound Josephine, the maid who sets the table and seats all diners, though she doesn't cook, hands akimbo, mouth open and gawking at the food.

"Josephine?" said Rosetta. "Is something wrong?"

"Ma'am? Look at the food. All spoil!" she answered, quite vexed.

"What do you mean, 'all spoil'?"

"Well, Miranda just cook the food. I dish it out. I put it on the table. And now it smelling!"

"Smelling?" Rosetta sniffed and found it to be true. The food was all spoilt. Clyde didn't seem to notice anything wrong. He lifted the covers from the rice and stewed beef and chicken. Then the macaroni pie.

"Seems all right to me." He tasted the gravy from the stews. "Yes. It's fine. Just as I remember."

He rubbed his belly and sat down to eat.

"Clyde!" she yelled at him. "That food is no good. You can't eat that. Don't. You'll get sick. Food poisoning or something worse." She held his hand to prevent him from tasting it. In return, he grabbed hers so tightly that she screamed, his face twisting in such a grotesque manner, as to be unrecognizable.

"You're hurting me," she said softly.

Clyde briefly let go, and his face was normal again, but only for a moment, then he was evil again.

"Shut up, you old hag, or I'll break your arm," he growled and slowly rising from his seat, seemed to have sprouted two inches. Rosetta twisted her arm, freed herself, and with incredible strength, she had him on the floor with her foot on his chest. With her index finger and little finger pointed at his face, she whispered something unintelligible. Clyde remained quiet and immobile. The strange earthquake came again, only this time it was furious and its anger directed at Clyde, lying prone on the floor, rolled him and slammed him against the walls. Miranda came in at that moment and seeing the frozen expressions on the faces of all gathered there, knew she had to do something. She took the dish of stew, noticing the maggots within, and slammed it onto Clyde's face, simultaneously telling Rosetta to remember.

Unnoticed by all, the maggots penetrated Clyde's body, and he got up with his back stiff and marched out of the room.

"Remember what!" she exclaimed.

"Stop thinking so much. Shut off your thoughts and you'll know what to do."

The wind was getting stronger and louder, and the maids huddled in a corner, hugging each other and apparently praying.

Rosetta closed her eyes and spinning slowly on one spot, asked for the lota and large brass bell from the cupboard.

Miranda dutifully got them, and Rosetta filled the lota with water from the goblet. She threw some to the east, then west, then south. Ringing the bell that belied the strength of her small frame, she stomped along the corridor in the direction of the secret rooms. Smoke filled the dining room area, and the outlines of people were apparent. But they weren't people, they were the ghosts of Charuma Forest, and they were angry—very angry.

"Where is Garrison?" they asked in unison.

"You know where he is," Miranda answered.

"His daughter is shielding him." They hit back with a force.

"No, no. It is she who called you here. To protect and defend the house and all therein. We're under attack. Again. This time by Garrison." Miranda spoke as though with someone who is familiar to her.

"No. Where is Garrison?" they asked again.

"Follow the sound of the bell," she stated, whereby they promptly vanished.

"All of you. Go to the safe room. Where is Josephine?"

"She ran out when the ghosts came in."

"All right. You all go ahead. Whatever you hear, don't come out. And don't open the door. You won't die, but you'll wish you did."

In the rush to get to the safe room, they didn't see Josephine come in with what appeared to be a galvanized bucket that was quite heavy. Miranda also did not see her. She was busy gathering more stuff from the various cupboards. The screaming started as soon as she uncovered a certain pot that was smoking. Or the contents was just evaporating. She wasn't sure which. She raised her eyebrows and with a satisfied expression, hustled to where she expected the ghosts to be.

Seeing Rosetta tied to a chair, she hid behind a cupboard and with the wooden spoon, stirred the smoky contents of the pot. The ghosts of Charuma forest solidified while the body of Clyde, temporarily housing Garrison, dropped to the floor with a loud thud.

"Ouch!" Clyde exclaimed. Opening his eyes and shocked at the scene before him, he scrambled to the nearest wall and hugged his knees. The golden pieces were strewn all over the floor and had lost their sheen. Seeing his grandmother tied to a chair and Miranda hiding behind the cupboard with her finger to her lips, he knew he should keep quiet.

At that moment, Rosetta caught the eyes of Miranda, who pelted the pot at her at the same time shouting, "Hit it a butt!"

Alert and fast, the butt sent it flying to Garrison, who was just materializing. It went through his belly, spinning him a bit, so he ended up with his feet turned backward. The ghosts, with hands outstretched and a deep angry growl, went straight for him. He tried to vanish but couldn't. At the same time Josephine came with the galvanize bucket that was too heavy for her to throw to him. The contents spilled, and Garrison melted away.

Rosetta got loose from the chair and clapping her hands while uttering some unintelligible words, brought back the spirit of Garrison, who again tried unsuccessfully to vanish.

"Oh no you don't!" she squealed as she apparently drew an unseen dagger from her waist and sliced him twice, left and right. "This is for my mother." Then she sliced off his head, saying, "And this is for my grandson."

The ghosts of Charuma forest methodically returned all the gold pieces to their rightful place then vanished. The ghost of Marie, Rosetta's mother, materialized as a young woman with the same dress she wore the night of her disappearance. With a charming smile, she gazed at her daughter and great-grandson and mouthing "thank you" she left.

UNHOLY TEACHER

"They say if you point a safety pin at their back without them knowing you're there, and they turn around, it means they do turn into a chicken or a goat or something."

"Say what it is. Soucouyant." Marla, the oldest, was as forceful as ever.

"Don't say that word. They'll come get you." Joan was the opposite, always careful not to offend.

"Don't be silly. That's old wives' tale."

"What is an 'old wives' tale'?" Little Johnny, bringing up the rear, was always ready with a question no matter how obvious.

"Made-up stories to keep us children in line."

From her vantage point, nestled between the thick branches of the silk cotton tree, Amelia watched and listened to the children's arguments about ways to recognize a soucouyant, and it brought a smile to her face as she remembered her own childhood days.

Admittedly they were stories back then, but as she grew older, she acknowledged the reality of it all. That reinforced her desire to leave for brighter and greener pastures where no evil beings existed, but simultaneously caused her to remain in the mountainous region among her family.

On that fateful day, she'd misjudged the time and was subsequently late in leaving her friend's house on the other side of the hill. Darkness enveloped the area between the hills quite early in the evening, and as she stealthily made her way through the darkened ravine, scared of the slightest sound, she was petrified by the sudden appearance of two women whom she knew.

First, the silhouettes of the trees were barely discernible, then there they were, giggling like teenagers, holding hands, and jumping about like rabbits. Amelia stood there transfixed at the sight, not knowing which way to direct her thoughts. Then the unthinkable happened. There was a cloud of smoke for a few seconds, and when it cleared, two goats were in the place of the women. Amelia hid behind the closest tree but not before her presence was felt by them. Peeping from the side of the tree, she witnessed the goats placing something huge in a crocus bag while swivelling their heads, apparently searching for the scent of the regular human.

Not seeing anyone, they continued their task, and hefting it on to the back of one of them, they sauntered out of the ravine.

Amelia raced home at breakneck speed, rushing into the house, slamming the door after her. Dropping onto the floor breathless, she could feel the eyes of her parents and siblings on her.

"Amelia? What happened to you?" her older sister asked.

"Girl, I just see two soucouyant. And I run home as fast as I could. No, don't open the window," she shouted at another sister. "They may have seen me. And they'll come for us."

"Amelia, if they are coming for us, a locked house won't stop them." They all swivelled to face their mother, who was calm as she dried her hands with the dirty kitchen towel. "They can also turn into something quite small and insignificant, like say a cockroach, and come through any crack in the house."

"This is a board house, Mom. There are more cracks than anything else. What do we do?" Terrified of the unthinkable, the children stared at their mother, waiting, hoping.

"Get the smallest calabash from the back room. Amelia, you get the holy water from the altar, and, Ronnie you put on your father's long black coat."

"But, Mom! Dad is six feet tall. And I am only four feet six. It will swallow me. What good will that do?"

"It will serve its purpose."

Rushing to perform their tasks, they didn't notice the smoke appearing outside the window on the southern side.

When it cleared, the two goats were in place. They looked at each other and bobbing their heads, turned and went in opposite directions. Inside the house, the mother, in the act of preparing a concoction with the holy water and other stuff in the calabash, while turning on one spot, tripped on a rolling marble and fell, dropping the calabash and spilling the contents. Ronnie came out from the bedroom wearing the coat and shocked at seeing their defense spoiled, couldn't utter a sound. The two goats made a frightened sound and vanished at the sight of the coat.

"What will we do now, Mom?" Ronnie whispered. "Where are Amelia and Jessica?"

He spotted them cowering in a corner and admonished them. "This is no time to be cowards. Dad's not here to defend us. We have to be brave and remember all we were taught and help Mom. Now get up, shake yourselves, and let's get these things away from our house."

At the force in his voice, they got up prepared to fight for their lives and souls.

"Okay, Ronnie. At the sound or your voice, they now know you're not the owner of the coat. Take it off and start praying all the prayers you can remember."

The entire house started shaking like an earthquake was in progress. The cupboards toppled over, and all the wares shattered.

"Careful, don't get cut. It won't heal. You'll have a lifetime sore foot," said their mother.

Amelia, shaking from head to toe, shuffled to the kitchen, where she collected a container of salt and threw it out the window, hoping to catch at least one of the invaders. A loud painful growl proved her success. Their mother shouted from the other room.

"Amelia, you all right?"

"Yes, Mom. I threw some salt," Amelia shouted back.

"Good. It's coming to you."

The salt had an unexpected result. It stung so much the goat reverted to its human form and couldn't walk. They recognized Lillian even though she had no skin.

"Lillian? You? Why you trying to harm my family?" Amelia asked, shocked.

"We were just having some fun," Lillian answered as best she could with her skinless mouth.

"By trying to give us a heart attack? Get out of here."

Barely able to walk, Lillian crawled out.

"Where's Ronnie? Ronnie!" she called, but she go no answer. He turned up sometime later and explained his disappearance.

"I went to Lillian's house and found the mortar where she left her skin. I saturated it with salt and hid for when she came back to put it on. Mom, I've never heard so much screaming since the day I born. Talk about scream!"

"Why did you do that? It wasn't a very nice thing to do," his mother admonished.

"And what she did was nice?" Ronnie hit right back.

"Two wrongs don't make a right."

"Mom, they knew Dad wasn't home. They didn't come to play. They came to hurt."

"Okay, I understand. But it's still wrong!"

They spent the rest of the night huddled together in fearful anticipation of what the other goat may do in retaliation for the horrible end meted out to her partner in evil doings.

At daybreak, they were rudely awakened by a rowdy commotion outside the house. Ronnie peeped through a crack above his pillow and was shocked to see the rowdy crowd of people with sticks and stones, quarrelling at the top of their lungs and hurling abuses at their household. He carefully roused his mother and siblings, shushing them to be quiet. He pointed outside where the unruly crowd were just about to throw stones at the house. Their mother flung aside the bed sheets, sprang from the bed with the apparent energy of a teenager, and pushed open the door with such a force as to unhinge it. Hands akimbo, she faced the crowd who grew silent at the fierceness of her countenance. The stones dropping with a slight pop, they all tried to hide behind each other, none wanting to be in the frontline. Even though they all knew each other, they'd never seen her angry. She'd always be one step behind her husband, and he always did the talking. This action of hers reminded them of the saying "Don't mess with a mother hen's chicks."

"What do you think you're doing?"

"It was Ronnie, Mrs. Holloway. He killed Lillian. She was one of us."

"Tell me how, where, and when, and I'll deal with him. You have no authority here. Understand?"

"I heard her screaming," a squeaky voice said from the back.

"And I saw him running from the house," said another.

"And we went in her house, and she was—"

"Was what? Please continue. Was what?"

Since none answered, she chased them away with a broomstick, threatening to beat the life out of at least one of them.

Hearing the giggles, she gave her offspring one of her looks, and they all froze. But not for long.

"Mom, you were great."

"We didn't know you had it in you."

"Well, with your father away, someone has to be the big bad wolf. Might as well be me. And we're not done yet. They'll be back."

"Mom, why are they defending Lillian? She hurts everyone."

"Well, children, everyone's got their fan club, and so does she. Who's the other goat, Amelia?"

"Teacher Mary."

"The school principal?" Mrs. Holloway, shocked out of her wits, was now at a crossroad. "What do we do now? My goodness." She sat on the closest chair, folded her arms, and rocked feverishly. "Teacher Mary. She's responsible for the education of all the children in the village."

"We'll get another teacher, Mom."

"No outsider will take a post here."

"Why, Mom?"

"Because of the amount of Lillians we have here in our midst. Only we could handle our own."

"But why do they do it? They born so?"

"No. It's a skill they acquire. They choose it and learn it. Like a subject in school."

"Is there any way to stop them?"

Mrs. Holloway's expression suddenly changed. She snapped her fingers and exclaimed, "That's it!" She jumped up from the chair and issued instructions like it was going out of style.

When all was ready, she sent Amelia to the corner shop with a grocery list.

"Just do it and shut up." Mrs. Holloway was very good at rebuking in advance.

The message hidden in the grocery list had the desired effect. In no time at all, the rowdy gang was at the Holloways' gate.

"They're back. And we're dead."

"No, dears. I sent for them?"

"How? You didn't send any of us out. Only Amelia to the grocery."

"Yes. I put in a secret message that would get them all here, including the cow disguised as a human. We have to end this cycle once and for all."

Not knowing what's on their mother's mind, they waited patiently while she positioned the chairs in a specific order around the room.

"Invite them all in. Have Teacher Mary sit on this chair."

Doing as they were told, the guest were comfortable but quiet and kind of humbled. Teacher Mary sat in her assigned place and soon started to scratch. First, her arms then legs and back. She twisted and turned this way and that and then came the screams.

"Teacher Mary? Is something wrong?" asked Mrs. Holloway.

"Uhh, I t-think some stinging nettle must have gotten into my clothes somehow. I've g-got a terrible itch all over," she stammered her answer.

"That's terrible. I'll get you some balm."

Mrs. Holloway handed her a bottle of something that resembled orange juice.

"Thank you." She poured out a handful and plastered her arms with it, then another and another in quick succession. Within a few minutes, the blisters made their appearance. Everybody screamed and watched Mrs. Holloway with such hatred in their eyes the children froze. Mrs. Holloway, on the other hand, was calm and collected.

"Now you will never change again. You shouldn't have taken that man to be sacrificed."

"What are you talking about?" the guests asked in unison.

"The one you put in the crocus bag. You shouldn't have. He was my half brother, dim-witted but still my brother."

"You did that?"

They all turned on the teacher, but she was already spoiled. She could never turn again. Her skin was broken.

MANGLING DONE HERE

Moses stabbed the tabletop with the long wooden-handled knife that his wife gave him for his last birthday.

From the adjoining room, Stella cringed as she visualized another mark on her well-loved table. A genuine article handed down to the first child from each generation. An heirloom that tells a story. Made by an ancestor with his bare hands, in such a way that each succeeding owner can carve their own story into the legs or wherever takes their fancy. No machinery existed in those days.

"Dammit, Moses!" she exclaimed, too softly for him to hear. "One of these days I will ram that knife into you."

She regretted giving it to him like she never regretted anything in her life, but she loved him and knew he needed that knife like one needs air to live. Going into the room referred to as the prayer room, she bowed in front of the statue of one resembling St. Michael, patron saint of warriors. She asked for guidance in this new realm of wife's duties to the husband, when to fight and when not to. When is it disobedience, and when is it protection of one's rights? She didn't expect an answer. None had ever been proffered.

"Honey?" she heard her husband calling out to her and didn't answer. "Oh, sorry," he said, and walked out.

Finished with her daily oblations, she went to the kitchen, where she found her husband in a state of distress. Still fuming from the earlier incident where he damaged her table, she feigned unconcern, deliberately turning away from him.

"Yes, dear, you wanted me?" she asked.

"Sorry for disturbing you. Didn't know," he answered softly.

"Forget it. Wanted something?" Stella was more rough than she wanted.

"It's my sister, Stella," said Moses.

"Chloe?" She faced him then and saw the deepening lines on his forehead and the pulsating vein that always meant trouble on the horizon. "What's wrong with her?"

"It's her husband. He walked out on her three weeks ago. Moved in with that woman two streets down. And in her family's house too. What kind of people takes another woman's husband to live with their daughter in their own house? Under their roof?" He was rocking on the stool, signs that he was trying to keep his anger in check.

"One with low morals," Stella stated. "And Chloe?"

"She's humiliated, Stella. Oh, the pain and trauma that she's undergone, Stella. And she didn't tell me."

"How did you find out?" curious, she inquired, afraid of the answer.

"Accidentally. In the public toilet in the savannah. I couldn't make it home, so I went in there. There were some men around talking and laughing. Didn't pay them no mind until I heard Stanley's name. I stayed there until they left. I wanted to go straight to her, Stella. But I know what I'm capable of, and I promised your father I'd behave myself and not cause you any worry, so I came straight home." Moses sat on the kitchen stool, rocking back and forth, and Stella was amazed at how he succeeded in keeping his temper in check.

"Thanks for that, Moses." She heaved a sigh of relief. "How about I go and check on her?" she offered.

"What good will that do? She loves that man so much."

Stella felt that love for her husband again. That first time when she saw him gentle and kind. He had taken up a puppy that was left at the roadside. It was shivering from cold and hunger and whatever else. He wrapped it in his jacket that did look new, without a second thought. He didn't see her, of course, because she was wearing her camouflage outfit on her way to her favourite pastime of hunting. That season just reopened a month before.

Now, he rocked back and forth on the stool in the kitchen, knife in hand and holding his head.

"Three weeks. That's a long time. I'll fix some food and make some groceries and take it to her. Do you think she'll be at home now?" Stella asked.

"I don't know. She used to work in that restaurant on the promenade. Used to drive herself there, but Stanley took the car."

Stella fixed her husband a cup of tea, and armed with sustenance for her sister-in-law, she left, locking the door behind her. She was careful to leave all sharp instruments hidden away.

Stella and her family were well known far and wide. Nobody would mess with them, especially Stella. Not after seeing her wield an ax. She came through the glass doors of the restaurant as quiet as a mouse and wasn't seen till she was close to the bar section. The owner came across to her as fast as his eighty-year-old legs would allow.

With a smile reaching from ear to ear, he greeted her with a chirpy sound, "And what can we do for you today, Miss Stella?"

"I'm looking for my sister-in-law. Is she here today?"

"Every day as usual. She's out back. Next to the dumpster."

"Why the dumpster?" Stella asked, incredulous.

"It's quiet, she says. No one goes there except at closing time to take out the daily trash. You understand? She can't help but cry. All day long. So sad. Stanley should never have done what he did, Stella." Mr. Jonas, in his concern for Chloe, whom he knew since birth, as well as her parents' births, refused the offer of Chloe's salary to be paid by Stella, unknowing to her brother.

"That bad, huh. Thanks for not telling Moses. But he just found out." Stella lowered her voice to a whisper.

"Help her. Please. All we can do is sympathize. She needs practical help." Mr. Jonas showed his concern and inability to do anything worthwhile to help.

"Send her brother after that family, Stella. What's wrong with him? Gone all soft in his old age?" interjected a patron who overheard a snippet of the conversation.

"Shut up and mind your own business, Caleb. Aren't you the one responsible for bringing those outsiders here in our midst?" Mr. Jonas hit back.

"I'm sorry about that. Thought they were decent folk. They'll be on the other side of the hill next weekend," Caleb whispered. "They just bought O'Briens' place as a getaway."

"I'll go check on her." Stella pointedly ignored Caleb and went out back, where she found Chloe sitting on the ground, cross-legged and facing the dumpster. The picture of total dejection, her unwashed hair matted like a newborn donkey. A surge of sympathy rose within Stella's chest, threatening to erupt in a blast of rage. Stella touched her shoulder, calling her name so she wouldn't get startled, which just could result in a heart attack.

"Chloe?" she said gently. "Let's fix this. You can't go on this way."

Chloe turned to her, hope written all over her face. "What can I do, Stella, if he doesn't want me?"

"No, no, I think it's more than that. Maybe he was drugged or something."

"I could handle him being unfaithful. I cannot handle his not loving me or wanting me anymore." A fresh flood of tears bathed her face again.

"Come on. Get up. We're going home. To my place."

"Your place?"

"Yes. Moses will take care of you there. Don't worry about a thing. You'll be fine. After all, you are my favorite sister-in law."

"I'm your *only* sister-in-law." Her face lit up a bit with a bright-ish smile, and Stella felt confident that all was not lost.

With Chloe settled in the house with Moses, and instructions on what to do and what not to do, Stella prepared for the task ahead. A few minutes later, Moses followed her into the garage. He found her in the process of zipping up the black bag she used only when going off to cut down trees, Moses visibly stiffened as that all-too-familiar sense of apprehension welled within his stomach and reflected on his face.

Stella paused then said, "Don't let her out of your sight, Moses. Okay? She's kind of fragile right now, and she may try to hurt herself."

"Yeah, I know. But what are you going to do, Stella? And don't tell me you're going into the forest to fell some tree or the other." He was unusually calm, just standing there with his hands dangling at his sides.

"My dear husband, I love you and respect you, and I don't want you to break the promise you made to my father, okay? One of us has to stand up for Chloe, and it can't be you. That leaves me. I didn't promise anyone anything. Now go watch your sister. You've already been away too long." He knew she meant business, and there was no stopping her when she is in that place. He watched calmly as his wife strapped on the bag, feeling totally helpless.

Moses, a shadow of his former self, meekly walked out of the garage, leaving his wife to her cause, confident she could handle herself. Stella, on the other hand, wasn't so sure about her husband babysitting his sister instead of doing what he does best. But she had no choice. Boots buckled up, bag on shoulder, she grabbed the cutlass case with her trusty screwdriver also intact and set out to right some wrongs the only way she knew how.

With the screwdriver, she loosened the screws from the back door of the cabin set in a lonely area close to the river, where Caleb said they'd be. She set up good and proper and waited. In no time at all, Mr. Hackshaw came through the front door, and she whacked him back of the head. He dropped like a leaf, and she proceeded to tie him up on the chair positioned for that purpose. Barely finished securing him, his wife entered. Same done to her, but she remained under for a lot longer. Stella made herself some coffee and sat down to enjoy it while contemplating how exactly she's going to torture them without killing them.

"What did I do to you, Stella?" asked Mr. Hackshaw, surprisingly calm, after first looking around the room and assessing the situation.

"You accepted Stanley under your roof. To live with your daughter. You do know his wife is my sister-in-law?"

Mr. Hackshaw, taken aback at the level of animosity in her voice, visibly trembled and was frightened as he remembered seeing her swing an ax in the forest when her father was alive and teaching her. She was a formidable enemy.

"I had nothing to do with that. You have to believe me. And I only found out today."

"You expect me to believe you don't know what goes on under your own roof? Don't insult my integrity. You're accountable." Spittle was foaming at the corner of her lips, and he decided against trying to save himself from her fury.

The sound of laughter from outside the house brought him out of his sad sack story.

"That would be my stepdaughter and Stanley. Take him and let her go. Please."

"If you had to choose an outsider for a wife over one of us, you could at least have chosen one with the same values. Quiet," she ended, and peeped through the curtains.

For the third time, she walked across to the kitchen, and he was prompted to ask the reason.

"You'll know soon enough." Brief and to the point.

Stanley and Bella strolled through the door, arms locked in a loving embrace and smiling into each other's faces like a couple of teenagers. It was sickening. Stella grunted as she hit Bella in the stomach with a two-by-four, the equivalent of a big truck ramming into a closed gate. Down she went and was cold before hitting the floor. Out of respect for Chloe's love for Stanley, she wasn't as hard with him. She faced him, her features as hard as granite, sending shivers up his spine.

"You!" she said, waving a finger at him. "Put on those gloves and tie up the man-thief with the barbed wire."

Stella was cold, heart apparently under lock and key. Stanley hesitated with gloves on and wire in hand.

"What's wrong, Stanley? Want some help?" Her voice as sweet as the sparrow.

"I'm sorry, Stella…" he started to explain but froze at her stone-cold expression. Her lips were so tight they formed a straight almost invisible line. "I…I…I can't do it. My…my…hands are trembling. See?"

"Give me that damn thing!" She stomped across the room to him and grabbed the barbed wire with her bare hands. Stanley stood transfixed while the father smiled, sure that Stella's hands would be ripped apart from the sheer force of her action. But no, she was skilled in the art of using such with her bare hands, and tying up Bella was child's play.

By now Bella was awake and frozen from the pain and shock of what was about to happen. Stella's facial expression was transformed into something so ugly and hateful that father, mother, and daughter were all screaming at Stella for mercy. Now silent and with movements as swift and stealthy as an animal, she collected a pot from the kitchen. Watching the steam rise from it, Mr. Hackshaw could only guess at the contents. He glanced at his wife and daughter and swiftly turned away.

Mrs. Hackshaw screamed, "No! Please don't do it! She's only twenty-five." With tears streaming down her face, she watched helplessly as Stella poured the contents over Bella's feet from the knees down. It didn't take long for her to get unconscious. Her stepfather noticed the consistency of the contents was not like water pouring. He asked, "What is that, Stella?"

"Sugar water." Stella was short and her voice brittle. Stanley tried to sneak out, but Stella lassoed him with the donkey rope that she had around her waist.

"Don't! Get back in that corner and sit until I decide how best to punish you." Soft and deadly, she continued pouring till done.

Stanley was confused as to how he ended up in this position. He tried reaching out to Stella, who'd always been good to him. "Please hear me out, Stella." He whimpered.

"Shut up, Stanley," she answered as she swung her attention to the mother.

"No. No. Please don't. Help! Somebody help!" she screamed.

"Nobody to hear you. This place is terribly isolated. Isn't that why you bought it? Now let's enjoy the seclusion." Stella raised her head to the heavens like a chicken drinking water and guffawed like a man, which only served to bring on more screams, now including the father. Using the pliers she brought with her, she proceeded to extract teeth. Using a contraption fashioned out of bits and pieces of cutlass wire and scrap metal that could only be found in the backyard of a country dwelling, she prized open and kept open her victim's mouth while she jerked and pushed and pulled and twisted their teeth till they were all out. First, the incisors, which weren't as difficult as the canines and the molars. Amid the blood and spittle secreted by the victims, as well as their screams, Stella was on a high. She didn't expect to feel as though she'd had some whiskey and coconut water, but she did. She enjoyed it to the fullest.

She wiped the sweat from her forehead with the back of her hand and exclaimed, "Whew! That was hard work. More difficult than felling a tree. You know that's what I do, right? And yet you chose to mess with my sister-in-law? You people are stupid for spite." She slapped Bella across the cheek before sitting on a stool, presumably to take a break while she mentally devised other ways and means to make them suffer for hurting Chloe.

"Looks like you could all do with a nice, nice pedicure." She looked at the three in turn and was mesmerized at the intense fear in their eyes. She smiled and continued, "What do you say?"

Their gums swollen to bursting point, they couldn't muster an answer.

Going across to Bella, she slapped her face again, though gently, and on her opening her eyes, she asked, "Didn't you hear me? Why not answer? Okay, I'll take your silence as consent. Pedicure it is."

She lifted both her feet, pretending to be examining the toenails. "Hm. I think we should first remove these ones, grow new ones, and then we shall see about pedicure. Okay?" She spun the pliers with her index finger, deep in thought. The stepfather dreaded what was next to come. If that was at all possible.

He knew that nothing would make Stella deviate from her purpose. And she was hell-bent on destroying his entire family herself in order to prevent her husband from breaking the promise made to her father. What a mess! Though he was in terrible pain, both mentally and physically, he empathized with Stella and wished for death.

"Stella, I'm no use alive," he mumbled as best he could with terribly swollen and painful gums. "I have no say in my own house, and now I am suffering for that. Please kill me and done with it." He tried pleading for himself only.

"You are—" Stella stopped in midsentence as the door flung open with such a strong breeze that she swirled to see who or what caused it.

There was Moses, face unrecognizable, twisted into an ugly grimace from which no words would form. He grunted and raved in some unknown language that could only be grief. He swung the cutlass and sliced of the head of, first, the father, who had no time to be grateful for the release from this world of torment, and then the mother. Finally getting ahold of herself, Stella grabbed his arm and swung it away from Bella, who was screaming with whatever was left of her mouth.

"Get a hold of yourself, Moses. Remember your promise."

"I'll apologize later, Stella." Tears streaming down his cheeks, he said, "Chloe is dead, Stella. My sister is dead. And they killed her." He pushed aside his wife and attempted to stab Bella, but she again foiled his attempt. Stella hugged her husband, who was totally out of his mind. But he freed himself and pushed her with such force that she catapulted over and across the table with Bella on it and ended up on the other side of the room. She somersaulted and was on her feet in two twos and back at her husband's side. Holding him in a neck grip, she spoke soothingly to him, "What happened? Tell me."

"She just stopped breathing." With those words, he elbowed Stella in the stomach and reached for Bella. While Stella was getting her bearings, he used the pliers to snip the barbed wire that was holding down Bella and had time to fling her hard against the wall before Stella got to her feet.

Ultimately he sat on his haunches, tired mentally more than physically, then started laughing.

"Chloe is free. My sister is free," he repeated while laughing. Then crying, he said, "My sister is dead. They killed her." Alternately laughing and crying, he repeated the words till Stella, at her wit's end as to what she should do, slapped him hard on the cheek. With a blank expression, he looked at his wife and said, "You killed Chloe. You killed my sister." He choked Stella, who tried unsuccessfully to free herself from his grip until her hands fell lifeless to the ground. Stanley, the reason for all the pain, heartache, the spilling of blood, and torture, tried to sneak out before Moses could regain his senses. Too late, he turned to see the spinning ax just before it hit him in the forehead, splitting his head in two.

Two weeks later, Moses walked through the doors of the club aptly called The Hardest Hard. The patrons stood at attention and raising their glasses, simultaneously said, "Welcome back, Moses."

THE STRANGE HEIRLOOM

E ventually he had to give it up. He knew that. It was prophe-
sied. He knew a prophecy should not be ignored. But there
was no time frame. He tried to postpone the inevitable for as
long as possible. But time has run out. Now he must do it.

He reflected on the past three months. What he'd done and
what he hadn't done. What stood out was the fact that he'd fallen in
love. And he fell hard. An impossible situation to be sure, because the
object of his affections was a young married woman, whose husband
was a financially well-off old man who had dealings with the under-
world. He was untouchable and dangerous.

Jonathan gulped down the hot cup of coffee and flinched as
it scorched his tongue and throat. Humming his favorite tune, he
grabbed his briefcase and with a spring in his step, was out the door,
slamming it behind him. He was late for an interview with the newest technological company in town. It is central, and the pay package
promised to be competitive. Plus, there's lots of room for growth, not
to mention plenty of spare time for partying. After all, what is youth
for if not to eat, drink, and misbehave?

He knew whatever the outcome, he'll be partying the entire
weekend and wouldn't be home till maybe Sunday. So he emptied
the mailbox.

He frowned at the contents, an outdated cassette wrapped in
clear plastic, complete with player, which he deposited in the backseat
of his car, a blue Subaru of which he was quite proud. His father had
bluntly refused to buy him one or to loan him the money. Neither
was he allowed to take a loan from the bank. He had to work and
save for it. And now he is so proud of it that he couldn't thank his

father enough for the lessons he'd learned. Because of his determination and forbearance, his parents let him have the townhouse for a small rent, when they bought a house in the countryside where no fencing nor walls were needed and where they could lay back in a hammock in their backyard between two mango trees.

"License and registration please," the officer said to him.

"Yes, sir," he answered, handing over the documents. "What's the problem, sir?" he asked.

"Over the speed limit," the officer answered, writing feverishly in his little book.

"What?" Jonathan looked ahead as though seeing for the first time. "How? What?" He scratched his head in bewilderment.

He was clearly confused and disoriented. As luck would have it, the second officer turned up.

"Jonathan Mackenzie? Is that you? Haven't seen you since what...harvest ten years ago?"

Jonathan watched him with a frown. He did not know this man. He didn't just forget him or couldn't place him. He'd never met this person. And how in hell did he get to this junction? He remembered putting the cassette in the backseat of the car and then, blank. He looked at his watch that showed it was two forty-five. Then he noticed schoolchildren, lots of them running and playing, so he surmised it was afternoon. Where did the time go? He'd left home at seven forty-five. What did he do all this time? Did he keep his appointment?

He turned the car around and proceeded to drive back home.

He twisted his nose at the sudden scent of something putrid emanating from the interior of the car. He turned down all the windows, and it was gone.

"What on earth was that?" he asked aloud.

A disembodied voice answered him, "Are you referring to me?"

He pressed the brakes so hard that the car came to a screeching halt, and he jumped out of it as one would a bathtub where worms or suchlike had invaded one's special place. He spun to look back into the car and heard giggles behind him. The children were so close to him that his ingrown aversion toward the little darlings reared its ugly head, and he promptly jumped back in and sped away.

In the safety of his home, he inserted the cassette into the player and pressed Play. It started instantly.

"I do not know you, and I know you don't know me. You are a name from a phone book. I deliberately chose an address far away from my home, hoping against hope that you are a total stranger. I have something to say. A story to tell. But not to anyone I know. Such revelations either see you wind up in the loony bin or even in jail. Here's my story." The man's voice was husky and flat, but the words were pronounced with utmost precision. No accent was detected.

Jonathan loosened his tie and as was his habit, sat at his desk with pen and paper at the ready, prepared to give the tape his undivided attention.

"My name is John Smith, mediocre like my parents, who lacked imagination. I was an only child who never attended school. Whatever little I know was taught to me by the girl who lived next door. Yes, there was a 'girl next door.' She befriended me when I was about eight or nine years old and disappeared the year I turned fifteen, which was ten years ago. She was the cutest, bravest, sweetest thing you could imagine, a little princess straight out of a story book. Though at that time, I knew nothing about princesses and even less about books." Here was a long pause, then it began again.

"Please do not switch me off. Allow me to tell my story in my own way. My story is far from boring, if I should say so myself." This was beginning to sound like a confession of some sort. Jonathan listened attentively.

"What started me off on a downward spiral was a very simple thing. A little lift of my father's very bushy eyebrow. And you know how it is said that it's the last drop of water that cause the barrel to overflow? Well, that oh-so-subtle lifting of said eyebrow was the last drop. I felt my entire body draining of all emotions, my facial muscles relaxing, my brain devoid of all thought, and my body exploded. My body actually developed a mind of its own. I watched as this body stomped across to the barn, rough, but at the same time with no effort, move the heavy tools aside to get to the power saw. Me, John Smith, wasn't thinking. I was just an observer."

At this point, Jonathan made a move to get up, 'cause he wasn't sure that he wanted to hear any more of the pseudo confession. What would he do with it? Go to the police? No crime was committed. No, out of the question. They would definitely start investigating him. In which case, he would lose his job, his family, his home, his credibility—everything that he'd worked for would go down the drain. How do they phrase it? That he aided and abetted something in the commission of a crime? No. So what would be his next move after listening? But before he could even take one step away from the chair, this eerie voice, strained and yet guttural, came back on.

"Stay where you are."

He turned swiftly to face the door, expecting without expecting to see Everard, his friend from up the street, in the room. But there was no Everard. He sat back down. With trembling hands, he dried the beads of sweat forming on his forehead. Now he was definitely scared. Scared out of his wits. He gazed at the player. Nothing strange there. Just an ordinary player from a bygone era. But the cassette was also from a bygone era. Gosh, they stopped making these things years ago.

The voice continued, "As I was saying, while on my way to the room with all the tools, my eyes fell upon a little antique padlock all rusted with age, in a little corner about two feet from the floor. Now why would anyone put a drawer or a cupboard that close to the floor? I mean, you'll have to bend over to get to it, right? Silly. Anyway, as I was in control again, I bent for a closer look. It was really very old, and it didn't look like it was ever used, at least not for a long, long time. My parents probably didn't even know it was there. I did learn from the girl next door that the house and all that went with it was in my family for generations. I got a pliers and broke it open. Effortlessly, I might add. I prized open the little twelve-inch square door. The hinges were so rusted, they fell apart and disintegrated. Within that little cupboard, past the buildup of cobwebs and dust and what have you, I found a gold chain with a small heart-shaped pendant that was in pristine condition, along with a watch. You know the kind with a chain that hooks around the shirt button and the watch itself you put in your pocket? The pendant and a watch. Now I asked myself, why would someone hide such mundane stuff in such an inconspicuous place? That's it.

"When I opened the pendant, a force very much like a fist, hit me with such violence in my stomach, that I catapulted across the room and was temporarily disabled. When I came to, I was disoriented and with a whopping headache. I am sorry, this is taking longer than I expected. Please bear with me. I have had no schooling whatsoever. Not in the traditional sense."

At this point, Jonathan needed to get some water because he was so thirsty, his lips were parched. But he dared not move an inch.

"Yes. So I just hit the clock with the tip of my finger, a bit gentle, and I found myself outside the barn door, looking at a scene which I thought should have been my life. Don't know where that thought came from, but there it was. And I could feel the anger rising from within. In my chest, but with my brain there was no reason for anger. So you can understand my confusion amidst some mental anguish and what have you. There, in front of me, was a world within a world. This is the only way that I can describe it. This child about two years old, wearing what looked like a dress, all frilly and stuff, ankle length, and a woman, whom I assumed to be its mother, playing with him. She wasn't more than a child herself. And a man, also not more than a boy himself, looking on and smiling from ear to ear. They were a happy lot. The mother was walking backwards, with her arms outstretched, and calling to the child while laughing. The child, however, was not walking on the ground. He was actually floating a few inches from the surface of the earth. And he was giggling.

"Then they all fell down. The three of them. They just dropped. Have you ever sprayed flies? You see how they just drop and remain still? Well, that's how it happened. My stomach made some cartwheels. My mouth went dry."

The voice speeded up here and was more intense. Jonathan could feel the anger in that speech. And he felt it within himself. He was actually angry in sync with the voice. He scratched his throat and brought himself back to reality.

The voice continued, "Then there was anger. So furious. So intense. Couldn't understand why. I mean, it was just a picture. Like I said, a world within a world. Maybe it was past. Maybe it was future. Maybe it was an alternative world. Maybe even a parallel world. I don't know. But it did hit me in my stomach. Then these two other people walked out of the surrounding brush. The woman scooped up the baby and tied him in her apron, after making some mark on his forehead with her thumb. The man had a pickax and a shovel. Using the pickax, he dug a hole and put in, first, the woman, then the man. Then he shoveled the dirt over them. The two people who committed that dastardly act are my present-day parents. I recognized them after a while."

Jonathan noticed that he was sobbing. Was he actually crying?

"That entire episode was the most horrible thing that ever happened to me. And let me tell you, some unspeakable acts have been committed against me. But I didn't know it then. Only after I became enlightened was I made aware of such things. After all there was only me. And that girl. I could never forget that girl. I always remembered her, always thought of her. Shall we take a break? I know you want to. Go get yourself something to drink. But don't leave the house. I shan't be much longer."

Jonathan seized the opportunity handed to him as it were on a silver platter and got some coffee. He moved the drapes a bit and peeped out, but there was no one on the streets. No cars even. Where were people when needed? He contemplated making a dash for it, but felt silly thinking about running away from an old cassette player. He went back to his former sitting position, and the tape started rolling again of its own accord. The atmosphere in the room was now slightly different. There was heat and some buzzing, as though a hive of bees were suddenly out on their hunt. It was also sweet smelling. Too sweet for his comfort. But he had to bear with it. The flickering lights weren't a bother, but was a cause for concern. It could be faulty wiring, an overload, or just the effects of the cassette player and its eerie voice. Since he had no choice, he did nothing about it. He settled down to listen to the rest of it, hoping it wouldn't be much longer.

"Thank you for not attempting to make a dash for it. I know you thought of it. As I said, I won't harm you except if absolutely necessary. I do need you to get my story out there. You see, I think, though I am not too sure, that there are others like me. I just don't know how or where to find them. Besides, I've committed some dastardly and horrendous acts, though, of course, they were no fault of mine. I was compelled to do them. I'll explain them later.

"Let's see now. Where was I? Oh yes. My present-day parents buried the young couple and stole their child. I was feeling something for which I have no words to explain. Everything was incongruous with everything else. Feelings, sights, scenarios, and what have you. Even my sense of smell apparently went haywire. 'Cause now there were scents I'd never experienced before. Some were quite heavenly, others so stinky as to cause my eyes to spring water and my nostrils to burn. That brought on some heavy sneezing.

"I had never felt that way. It was new to me. But it wasn't a bad feeling. It was kind of powerful. I hit the watch again and was back inside the room. The real me. But I wasn't who I should have been. I grabbed the power saw and went into the house after my parents. My dad took one look at me and made a dash for his rifle. My mom slid open a cupboard drawer, keeping her eyes on me. That particular drawer contained only sharp and pointed instruments like knives and choppers. I believe there was also a hatchet in there. Now why would they do that?

"Simultaneously, they said, 'He knows.'

"Then it happened again. My body, with a mind of its own, sprang into action. It had to protect and defend itself at all cost. No matter the outcome. With no thought or questions of consequences, my body was propelled across the room with such force and speed, I swear I was in two places at one and the same time. First, I was at my mother's side, disarming her and hitting her, a disabling chop on the neck, taking away the chopper and flinging it aside, and simultaneously at my father's side, grabbing away the rifle before he could get a grip on it and twisting his arm so he remained bent over and howling like an animal in pain."

Everard chose that moment to knock on his door. Jonathan rushed to open it, hoping to get there before the voice intervened. He opened it with a gusto he didn't know he had. Grabbing Everard by the arm, he pulled him inside.

"Hold it! Hold it! I came of my own accord! What's with you, man?" Everard hollered and yanked his arm away. Watching Jonathan's expression of bewilderment, he showed concern. "Sorry. I didn't mean to yell. What happened to you? You look so scared," Everard continued.

Jonathan ran his fingers through his short curly hair and fumbling for words that wouldn't come, pointed to the cassette player. When no words were forthcoming, Everard prompted him.

"What's that? An old-time cassette player?" he asked.

"Yes. It talks."

"What do you mean it talks? That's what it supposed to do. Right?"

"No! It tells me to sit down. Stand up. It's haunted."

Everard laughed at him, and Jonathan cringed, realizing how silly that sounded. He paced the floor, mentally seeking the right words to explain his predicament.

"Here, Jonathan, come sit and tell me everything. From the beginning. Why do you think the cassette player is talking to you?" Everard placed Jonathan on the couch, but couldn't keep the grin from his face.

"Well, it's like this." He recounted the whole sordid affair from the start, and Everard was befuddled at the complexity of it all.

"Hmm. I don't know what to make of this. Are you sure of what you are saying?"

"Of course I'm sure."

"But I've been here for what, an hour? And nothing's happened yet."

"You're right. Maybe I blacked out and dreamt the whole thing? Yeah, that's probably it. Okay. You wanted to see me for something?" Instead of trying to convince Everard, he decided to change the subject.

"Oh, right. There's a party on at Carl's place. Want to come along? Chloe will be there." Everard got two beers from the fridge and handed one to Jonathan.

"Chloe? Are you sure?" Jonathan's face brightened as he accepted the bottle. "She doesn't go in for that sort of thing. Are you sure she'll be there?"

"Of course I'm sure. Tricia will be there too," Everard added.

"You can't leave. You still have to hear the end of my story," the gravelly voice from the cassette interrupted their conversation.

Everard spun this way and that way. "Where did that come from?" he shrieked.

"I wasn't dreaming. I told you," said Jonathan.

Everard dashed to the door but was stopped by the voice saying just one word.

"Tricia."

"What does it mean by that?"

"I don't know."

"Sit, both of you." After they were seated, it continued, "So where were we? Yes. I finished off my parents. Now I was in a quandary. Being myself again, I knew that I had done something that was against the law and possibly punishable by death. I'd learnt this much from the girl next door before she vanished from my life. Also, because windows were now opening for me, I couldn't afford to have them closed before I knew all about me. Who am I? Who are my real parents? Something out of a bubble is not good enough. What kind of a person am I? Those are the only questions I could have formulated at that time. And they were good enough and important enough, for me to seek answers."

"What is it talking about?" Everard whispered.

"No need to whisper, Everard. I can hear your words as well as your thoughts. You are Jonathan's best friend. You always have his welfare at heart, hence the reason you're here listening as well. He will need some help as well as support, and yours will be invaluable. I am telling him the story of my life. I need help, and he's the only one I find who is receptive to my way of communicating. So where were we? Yes. I need to meet my birth parents. I think they are in this world, but I'm not sure they are of this world. Don't ask what I mean because I don't know. Honestly I don't. Jonathan will fill you in, Everard."

"Mr. uh…What is your name?" Everard accepted it all like it was a normal everyday occurrence.

"You can call me Andrew." The voice now had a name.

"Okay, Mr. Andrew. What exactly do you want us to do?" he asked.

"This is where it gets kind of ticklish. I managed to retrieve a photo of my parents and put them in a file. Go check the top drawer of your bedside table, Jonathan. Stay where you are, Everard."

Jonathan was back momentarily with the file and a deep frown on his forehead.

"This is a girl and boy of about thirteen or fourteen, Andrew. How old are you? They won't be this age anymore."

"I still look like fourteen. That's what I mean by maybe we are not of this world. I don't sleep like others do. I move around quite a lot. I know I've been moving for about fifty of your years. I don't even know if they are alive. It's just a hope." His confidence was waning, and a sense of despondency was slowly creeping into his voice.

"This is somewhat of an impossible task," admitted Jonathan.

"Impossible for me, but not you two. I've devised a foolproof plan that would ensure getting desired results in the shortest time possible." His confidence was contagious.

"Let's hear it," the boys said together.

"I've got a distinct scent about me. Body odor, if you will, but not foul. Though it is totally different from anything you've ever experienced."

"What good is that?" Everard was indifferent.

"Hold your horses. Let me finish. I can transfer that scent to you. My parents will recognized it and hopefully approach you. They'll know you are not me, so my guess is they'll probably kidnap you to find out what happened to their son. This way, we'll find each other, and you'll have brought back one family from the brink of extinction."

"Sounds so silly it just might work. But do we just go walking about?" Everard was being quite realistic.

"You go about your daily routine. I think they are close at hand, hence the reason I was able to make contact with you, Jonathan. And now Everard can also hear me. After about fifty years in the proverbial wilderness, I see a ray of hope."

"Sounds easy enough. What do you say, Jonathan?"

"I don't see that we have a choice. After all, we are being controlled by an outmoded bit of technology."

"Okay then. Let's go to the party and have some fun. Something tells me we're not going to have that much longer."

Dancing with their partners and high from too much alcohol, Jonathan didn't notice the person who kept bouncing into him throughout the night.

Everard eventually did notice when she sniffed him, akin to a canine checking out his territory. Even though he was perturbed at the act, he said nothing but moved around the dance floor to escape her obvious advances.

Getting close to Jonathan, he whispered about the strange acts of the person. Jonathan ignored him. He was engrossed in the conversation he was having with his lady love.

"Listen to me, Jonathan!" he whispered kind of louder. "That girl is sniffing us."

"Nonsense. No one does that. It's disgusting." He shoved his friend away from him. The music stopped abruptly, and the same person brought them two drinks, which they accepted without a second thought or glance. They drank it up in one gulp.

They woke in a small wooden cabin with the sun streaming through the cracks. The small table in one corner was laid with a meal for two, judging by the plates and glasses. Jonathan sat up abruptly and slapping his head said to Everard, "I think there's something wrong with me."

"I'll say there is. With us both. Where are we?" he asked.

"I don't know. But I remember meeting a girl. And falling in love."

"Someone other than Chloe?" Everard asked, perplexed by this admission.

"Definitely. Young. Married. Husband a lot older." Jonathan started pacing the small room, oblivious of the strange surroundings. "I have to do something for her. For the life of me I can't remember what."

"Then you have nothing to worry about. But we do have this here and now. We don't know where we are."

A young girl, about fifteen, came in with such a serious expression and an air of doom that the boys got quiet and were apprehensive.

"You are not one of my own. I know because I can smell you. You've got our scent, but another as well." She spoke with conviction. "Who are you? And what have you done with my family?" she ended forcefully.

"Scent? Jonathan! This is she! Of whom Andrew spoke!" Everard jumped to the conclusion that this was indeed Andrew's mother.

"But she is so young," added Jonathan.

"Do not speak of me as though I am not present. Please," she said. "Do you know who I am?" she asked.

"Yes. But not quite. It's a long story." While Everard was speaking, she sat on one of the chairs as Jonathan stared openmouthed as he recalled this is the one with whom he'd fell in love. Reading his mind, the girl said, "It wasn't love, dear Jonathan, it was recognition. You are descended from a distant relative. Too distant to matter. You were chosen to bring us back from the wilderness to which we were banished. And separated, I might add," she explained. "My name is Shumaria. My husband is Micholo. And our son is Micholoson," she finished.

"Oh, so you know the story?"

"Most of it. I still don't know where my son is."

"Actually we've never met your son, per se. We know of him through an old-time cassette player, through which he communicated with us."

"I understand now. The prophecy. You were supposed to collect a bag from a certain shopkeeper, but you didn't. You chose to ignore what you were told and went partying. Right, Jonathan?" She faced Jonathan with such a fierce expression that he flinched.

"Sorry. I got no details. I know I should have done it, but there wasn't a time frame, so I thought it could wait."

"That caused my husband to age considerably."

"How can I make up for it? To make things right?"

"His aging is the result of a sickness, brought about by lack of a certain something that was in the package you should have delivered."

"Can I go back to that person and get another?"

"She's long gone. But maybe there is something. You communicated with my son through a cassette player?"

"Yes."

"Then he's evolved. Go back to him. Bring him here. To us. The prophecy can still be fulfilled. We'll all be together again. And my husband will be healthy."

"And those who buried you?"

"My son will take care of them. He thought he'd killed them, but he didn't. They cannot die. But I'd like you to prepare him for the shock he'll encounter when he meets us. Please tell him that the girl next door is me. I'll explain the rest."

And with that, she turned and walked out of the room.

Jonathan and Everard went back to Jonathan's apartment, and there they met a fourteen-year-old boy.

"Who are you? How did you get in here?"

"I am Andrew. You've freed me and my parents and brought us back. For that we are eternally grateful. Report to that company at which you had your interview. You've got the job. Thanks again."

Andrew vanished in the twinkle of an eye, but the sweet scent remained.

THE ANGELIC FACE

Andrew watched the girl coming his way and was mesmerized by her beauty. The long flowing gown and brown shoulder-length hair made him forget the stories that for the moment, seem farfetched. He approached her with the confidence of a precocious teenager. She was all too willing to accommodate him, and they were soon holding hands, walking, talking, and laughing.

Andrew didn't notice when her hair started growing longer and thicker.

Neither did he notice she had one human foot and one animal's hoof.

And she was taking him deep into the forest.

He didn't notice that he wasn't hungry nor thirsty.

What he did notice was palatial buildings and the most beautiful flora and fauna.

He also noticed the white goat grazing at the side of the road, which brought him back to reality.

Animals don't roam free in this community, especially at carnival time, when all hell breaks loose.

So Andrew asked the girl to pray with him. She released his hand with such force that it hurt him right where it was attached to his body.

She let out a bloodcurdling yell, her face twisting into the most horrendous monster, and on her head was now long wire strings instead of hair.

"You...you are the La Diablesse," Andrew stammered. He stumbled backward, tripped, and fell onto something that was slimy and moving. He screamed and jumped up with such agility that he surprised himself. He turned to see what moved beneath him, but stopped in his tracks when he noticed the wire strings coming at him to beat him. He believed the stories, now that it was almost too late. He continued praying but growing in crescendo, and in so doing, he inadvertently got his verses mixed up with nursery school rhymes.

The La Diablesse laughed at him. She had a lovely melodious laugh for one so hideous. He turned and ran into the darkness of the night, which threatened to swallow him up. He closed his eyes and tried to remember his father telling him to run with his hands closed as in a fist and he wouldn't stumble, neither would he miss a step. Now is a good time to try it out. It was working, but the La Diablesse wouldn't let him go so easily. The wind at his side let him know she was right there playing with him. Closing in for the kill. Andrew knew it would be futile to scream, he was surely out of earshot and miles away from civilization.

That's how the La Diablesse works.

He ran surefooted into nothingness.

He opened his eyes to see darkness all around him. His hands were tied to bedposts, and his entire body was burning as though he'd run through a field of razor grass, which he did, though he wasn't aware of it. He called out a hello, but his voice was raspy, and it didn't go far. The mattress was definitely made of fiber, and so lumpy he wondered just where he was. This was certainly some gardener's ajoupa, so he surmised that he was in the hills in a chive garden.

He wriggled a bit and to his surprise, found the straps loosening. He was soon free, and his eyes, getting accustomed to the dark, were able to make out the contents of the ajoupa. He made his way to the barrel, where he got some water. There was no moonlight, but he could recognize the dewdrops on the leaves of the fig trees. Pretty soon he heard the crowing of the roosters and knew it was foreday morning. Either one or two o'clock.

Being without a choice, he had to wait it out till sunrise. The La Diablesse had to have been long gone. He had no recollection of what happened after he ran headlong over a cliff.

He didn't have long to wait for answers. He heard the braying of a donkey and breathed a sigh of relief, because that says the gardener would soon be here.

"You're up. Quite an adventure you've had," he said on entering.

"Pardon me?" Andrew said.

"Your encounter with the La Diablesse. That talk is all over the village. You're lucky we found you. Two more days and you'd never be found." The gardener scared him with this revelation.

"What?"

"You young folks never listen when spoken to. I'm sure your parents told you not to approach any strange beautiful girl after six in the evening."

"Well yes, they did, but I didn't…"

"You didn't what? Didn't think they know what they were talking about?"

"Well, yes. Something like that," Andrew said sheepishly.

He was pounding something in the mortar using a pestle, and the scent was anything but pleasant.

"Oh well, I suppose I was the same at your age. Come on, get up."

He applied the stuff on Andrew's body, who screamed that it burned like fire.

"What happened to me?"

"The La Diablesse beat you with her hair. That's what they do. They don't like us men," he explained.

"You mean that's true?"

"Have you seen your body? What do you think did that?"

"Uh…uh, I don't know."

"She hypnotizes you into thinking you're in a civilized place while she takes you deep into the forest. With each giant step, her hair grows longer, and when it gets to her ankles, she beats you with it. By that time, it is wire. Hence the cuts. If you're found in a few days, you live. If not, well…"

"You're dead?"

"Don't know. We've never found a body, but we have lost a few young men."

"I'm never looking at another strange girl. No matter how beautiful. Only young men? Like me?" he asked.

"Yes. Older ones are wiser. We learn to look away," he answered.

THE GHOST PROTECTOR

H e first noticed the black car two days ago. Sure it was following him, he thought of who wanted him dead. He did do some horrible, regrettable things in his youth. Excusable, but apparently not forgivable. He swerved into side streets to get away, and just as he thought he was safe, there it would be again. Eventually he decided to take the bull by the horns. He stopped and walked the two car lengths ready for a confrontation. Knocking on the driver's side window and getting no response, he let out a string of colorful adjectives.

Turning to walk away, he heard the gentle hum of the window going down.

Through the light from the full moon, he saw the car was empty. He still bent and peeped for a closer look, but there was no person inside. And the door on the other side did not open. Maybe he missed it, and the person did sneak out the other side. "Oh well!" he said aloud, got into his car, and drove away.

There was the car again at his gate when he got home. He grabbed the length of iron he kept under the seat just in case of any untoward happenings.

Walking to his front door without another look at the car, the engine revved up, angry, like the roar of the ocean during high tide.

He turned with the upraised iron, ready to swing if necessary, but it stopped short of him, and headlights came on at full beam, blinding him for a few seconds. It revved up again, and Mario threw himself onto the hedge to escape. It stopped, and the most eerie, unearthly laughter emerged from the car as black smoke with the stench of a sewer being cleaned after umpteen years.

Trembling, Mario watched as it drove away and vanished into the night, swallowed up by the darkness around.

Knees knocking, he managed the few steps that got him into his empty house.

After a restless night, he got out of bed at five and peeped through a crack in his wooden shack, only to see his neighbor, old Mr. Mann, pussyfooting up the driveway and scratching his head in a funny sort of way. Mario called out to him from the open doorway and asked what's the matter.

"I see you've had a visit from our resident protector," he answered.

"What do you mean?" Mario asked, puzzled.

"All that blood," Mr. Mann said softly.

Mario raced down the three steps with a gasp and a shout. "What?"

"There. And there. See?" The old man pointed out the splatter of blood on the driveway and on the hedge.

"I didn't do that! It wasn't there last night."

"You came into contact with the protector and defender."

"What? Who?"

"What time did you come in last night?"

"About eleven thirty, I think."

"Anyone on the road?"

"No. I went to St. James to meet some friends for a drink. When I hit the streets here, it was a ghost town."

"Yes. Carla's on the prowl. You're breaking the rules. And she'll kill you."

"Who's Carla? And what rules?"

"She's our self-appointed protector and defender. She was killed by a drunken driver some years ago. Nothing came of it because his powerful father had some powerful connections. Out of grief, her father shot himself in the head a few months later.. But with his dying breath, he cursed the residents for not standing by him and his dead daughter. Since then this car would appear after ten at night. Two warnings and then she kills you. She runs you over with that black car. On the third night of her appearance, the car would be like that mangled wreck when she died. But it would be moving. So you, don't come home after ten and you'll be safe. You have seen it twice, right?" Mr. Mann questioned.

"That's all baloney. When you're dead, you're dead. End of story." And with that, Mario turned his back on the old man and walked away.

The following night, he again drove into the main road near midnight. He saw the car in the rearview mirror, and thinking he was well prepared for whoever it was harassing him, he led him to the savannah area, where there'd be no witnesses. He stopped the car and got out with his faithful length of iron ready to beat the perpetrator to a pulp. The car stopped, and that's when he noticed it was a wrangled wreck and should not be able to move. But it did move. He heard the engine rev up, and it came at him with such a speed he just barely got away by diving to the side.

The car spun on its side, swerved, and came at him again. This time he wasn't swift enough, and his right leg was crushed from his knee down. He screamed and called for help, but there was no one to hear him. He dragged himself toward the periphery, but being so far, the car had time to come at him again, this time crushing his left arm that he left on the ground while shielding his eyes from the blinding light with his right.

The black car drove about a hundred feet away, and feeling confident that he escaped death, he tried to get to his own car when he saw Mr. Mann.

He just stood there, hands folded, and with a grin on his face.

"Help me please," Mario pleaded.

"You were warned. Three times," he replied. "Look. My daughter is coming for you."

He pointed toward the car, and Mario was too shocked to utter a word. All he could muster was a slight groan as he watched the figure slowly emerge from within the twisted wreck. She was all bloody, and with her neck apparently broken, it was swinging over her shoulder. Her hands were stiff and horribly squashed. With one eye hanging from its socket, she approached Mario and in a gravelly voice, said, "No more deaths."

Then she was in the car again, which was now like it was the first time, and drove over Mario for the last time.

THE BLUE SMOKE

Marina was furious at her husband for not repairing the back step and causing her to fall on her haunches, hurting her pride and her dignity. Especially so as their sexually attractive and appealing nosy neighbour was just passing the house. She had the audacity to approach her, feigning concern. She had all the men at her fingertips. At her beck and call. And the wives are all too proud to show their jealousy or disapproval. So when Mario, her husband of ten years, showed up after work with all the dirt from the landfill still stuck to his clothes, it enraged her so much that she shouted at him.

With carving knife in upraised hand, about to chop the chicken for stewing, she stood transfixed, glaring at him.

"Mario! Get back out there with those filthy boots!" she screamed.

"Honey? This box was outside the door. Looks like a gift," he answered her calmly, unperturbed.

"I know. It doesn't say who from, does it?"

"No. So you mean I—"

"Yes, I do mean. It could be a bomb. Take it back out. Now."

Mario yielded to the temptation and as deftly and ably as he could, loosened the string with his rough and callused hands and sneaked a peek inside. There he saw a lovely white handkerchief. The whitest he'd ever seen. He always wanted a white handkerchief, but Marina insisted against it. Said it won't keep white. And a dingy white is the most disgusting thing to look at.

Mario installed the box under the patio seat, and the handkerchief he put in his pants pocket. He would not show it to Marina. Not for a few days.

She pays too much attention to the news. After all, it's not like they're living in a war zone. The terrorists are in lands too far away to matter. And he is just a garbage collector.

Still, he respected her feelings and her views on the issue. He admired and respected her concern for their welfare and safety. That was her first priority.

He strolled to the garden pipe, where he stripped of his boots and washed his feet before again entering the house. Marina smiled sweetly when he entered with clean feet and a sheepish grin on his face. He kept his secret close to his chest.

"You've got a choice today, Mario. Stewed chicken with pigeon peas and rice or curried chicken with dhal and rice?" she asked him.

"Curried chicken. We haven't had that for a while," he answered.

"How did things go today? Any problems?"

"No, just the usual. A funeral procession making it difficult to traverse the roadways. Don't they have anything better to do but die? There's a funeral procession every two days. That is a bother."

"Well, I don't think it is possible to make an appointment with death. So we'll just have to live with it."

Mario laughed at the irony of that observation.

"Hello, Miss Marina." The neighbours, two boys aged eleven and thirteen, came in. They are quite respectful, and Mario and Marina didn't mind that they visit from time to time.

"Oh, hello, Mike and Tommy. Where are you off to all dressed up so nice?" she asked them with a compliment.

"We came from the cemetery, Miss Marina. Mr. Lawrence was buried today," Tommy, the elder, answered.

Mike was a bit shy. Never talked too much. Even as a baby, he didn't cry much either. But their mother would be the first to say, "Still waters run deep." Mike is not to be trusted. The dog that barks never bite. That would be Tommy.

She fixed a dish with some cakes and sweets for them to take to their home, as was the custom.

"Those boys will make fine men someday. They'll make their parents proud."

"Yes. They are doing a grand job in raising them with respect and discipline. And they're doing well in school too."

"Why are you scratching so, Mario? Didn't you cover up yourself properly? You've been doing that since you finished dinner. And I know you're not allergic to the food I cooked."

"It's a strange itch, Marina. It's kind of a sticking under the skin. Like tiny needles, but it doesn't hurt. Just make me want to scratch. I'm not going to the doctor."

"I know, Mario. I know. We'll monitor it and see what happens between now and morning. For the time being, I'll get you some cream."

She was rubbing the cream when she felt a stinging sensation in the small of her back. "Ouch," she said and arched so suddenly that the cream splattered all over Mario's leg.

"There. You've gone and wasted good money," exclaimed Mario.

"Something stung my back. Felt like a Jack Spaniard."

"Nonsense. A Jack Spaniard can't sting through your clothes."

"I said it felt like one. Not that it was one."

Mike and Tommy heard the raised voices from their hiding spot within the hibiscus hedge. It was thick enough to conceal them both.

"That didn't take long," said Tommy.

"Told you," Mike replied. "Mr. Lawrence was always one to move fast. 'Never waste a second,' he used to say."

"But he just got an itch. What so scary about that? You said we'd see some fireworks as soon as he touched the handkerchief."

"Wait. You'll see."

They were both startled when a heart-wrenching scream burst through the air, and they fell backward into the hedge, causing such a commotion as to set the dogs barking.

They regained their position and on looking again to Marina and Mario, saw that Mario was hell-bent on scratching away his flesh. Marina was holding her face in her hands and screaming. He was sitting on a chair while Marina was standing a few feet away from him. The screaming stopped as Mario suddenly stood up straight as a soldier standing at attention, and he slowly dropped to the floor like all his joints did give way.

Mike and Tommy ran all the way home, screaming at the top of their lungs for their mother, who heard them and came out running asking what's the matter.

Breathless, and speaking together, they recounted what was happening next door.

But Tommy blurted out what they'd done with the handkerchief. That resulted in a kick from his younger brother.

"What? You did what? Who told you about that?"

"The kids at school. They said there'd be fireworks when anyone touches something from the dead."

"Fireworks? What kind of fireworks?"

"We didn't ask."

"You boys will be the death of me. Get in the house and stay there," she shouted at them.

Mrs. Headley practically ran to the phone and frantically dialed a number.

"Thank you. Then I'll see you day after tomorrow, at ten in the morning." She hung up and called out to her boys.

"You two will stay in the house for the rest of the week. No going outside. For no reason whatsoever. Is that clear?"

"But, Mom! We have school," they objected.

"For no reason. You've raised a hornet's nest, and now I have to clear it up. Get out of my sight. Go!"

Dejected, they went to their room, grumbling.

The next day Mrs. Mackenzie was punctual and got to work immediately. She dressed herself in a long black gown with a hood and set up candles in and around the house.

"We first have to protect your house before going to Mario's," she explained, while using the incense burner to smoke in and around the house. She was careful to include all crevices in her doings. When she was done, she asked for some water in a clear glass.

"This is to ensure that the spirit does not enter. Because he already knows what we're doing here, he will come. He knows who stole his handkerchief." The incense burner fell from her hands as she clutched her chest, grimacing in pain.

"What's wrong? Are you all right?" Mrs. Headley asked, concern in her voice.

"Pain. He's here!" she whispered agonizingly.

"Boys?" she called out. "I'm going next door to get Miss Clothilde. Something's wrong. Watch her."

"Miss Faslady already knows what's wrong. She's always peeping."

"Don't say that. Mom says don't. It's not nice."

"And I suppose I shouldn't call her Miss Faslady?"

"You're a pest. And always will be."

"She's always sticking her nose where it doesn't belong. Everyone says so."

Miss Clothilde, otherwise known as Miss Faslady, had nothing to do with her time, so she chose to be the unofficial watchdog for the community. Whatever is going on, she is sure to know.

At this particular moment, she was recounting to her long-suffering husband the doings of her neighbor's children, namely messing with the dead.

"Do you know what those children did?" she asked him, though it was not really a question. "They sneaked the white handkerchief out from the pocket of the deceased while he was lying there in his coffin."

Mr. John dropped the newspaper and stood on his feet as though propelled by something invisible. "What?" he exclaimed. "They did what?"

"Yes. And they gift wrapped it and laid it at the door of Mario and Marina."

"God Almighty! What on earth possessed those boys to do something like that?"

"You tell me. Their mother and everyone else are assured of their respect, discipline, and moral values. If you ask me, I'd say they are deceitful and hypocritical. The younger one more so than the older. They are quite demonic, that's what they are."

"You read too much into everything, wifey dear, but with the ever-present danger now, I think we'll need that inquisitive and downright disrespectful mind of yours."

Clothilde wasn't always a busybody like she is now. As a young girl, she was kind and considerate of others, minding her own business and not interfering with others. Not until she was accused of slandering the name of a student, and she couldn't prove her innocence. All and sundry went against her, to the detriment of her health and that of her parents', who went to an early grave. And to add insult to injury, only the priest and acolytes were present at the double funeral. Even the pallbearers refused to work on that day. Clothilde, an only child, had to resort to hiring, practically begging, men from outside the community to do the needful.

From that incident, a conniving, scheming, calculating, and utterly degenerate woman was born. And there was no turning back. She vowed to make them all pay for her sufferings. She didn't even choose a husband from the community. She got one from far away, one who is just as inconsiderate as she is now and treats others with total disregard and contempt.

Mr. John went into the bedroom to put on a shirt so he could at least show some respect for Mrs. Headley when she called at the door as he knew she would. Presently the expected knock arrived, with shouts of "Miss Clothilde," who answered, only too happy to refuse help of any kind. She was coughing terribly as she opened it, declining help due to ill health.

"Do you at least know who could counteract this spell put on Mario? It will affect everyone here. Mr. Lawrence wasn't a nice person. And as a ghost, I think he'll be worse," Mrs. Headley pleaded.

"God help us. Now he doesn't have to hide to do his mischief. But I didn't do him any harm. Did you?" Miss Clothilde's unkind remark passed unnoticed due to the state of confusion and frustration in which Mrs. Headley found herself.

"No. But it was my boys who took his handkerchief from his pocket while he was lying there in his coffin," she volunteered.

"Wasn't that Mrs. McKenzie I saw at your house? She is quite capable of performing that kind of ritual. She's been extremely successful so far. She did the job for the Phillips when their house was haunted."

"Yes. She dropped like a leaf while performing the ritual. It wasn't completed."

"My goodness. Now we're all in trouble!" She covered her face with her hands, and her body shook unashamedly.

"What do you mean?" Mrs. Headley asked, confused.

"Well, it's the forces that killed her. They don't want to be stopped. Now you'll have to get someone stronger. More powerful. Your boys sure did it this time around."

Mrs. Headley brushed the hair from her face, and in a daze, she spun once and then a second time, not knowing what to do or where to turn. She stooped right there in front of Miss Clothilde, who folded her arms and looked down on her with disdain and a satisfied smirk on her face. John, Clothilde's husband, was overcome with compassion at the sight of the dejected woman stooping there, crying her heart out. He couldn't help himself. He went and lifted her by the arms and hugged her, not looking at his wife, whom he knew would be scowling at him. But for once in his life, he decided to show some consideration for a fellow human being.

He hadn't felt like this in ages. Not since his father left for work when he was ten and forgot to return. His mother finally caught up with him five years later, living quite richly and comfortably with the siren from a neighboring town. He didn't have to work, but everything was provided for. His mother was devastated, but what made it worse was when she told her best friend in confidence.

That sheep in wolf's clothing unashamedly laughed in her face and told her it was all her fault. She was too high and mighty. And other stuff too disgusting to repeat or to remember. John was out of sight behind the fence repairing his broken bicycle and peeped at the sound of the laughter, which he had never before heard. And then he saw his mother crying. Her shoulders were shaking so much, and she slowly sank to the ground. As though from afar, he heard what was being said to his mother. He wanted to go to her, but some inner voice was telling him it's not the right thing to do. So he didn't.

Seeing Mrs. Headley on the ground brought back those terrible memories of helplessness and despair. He did the only thing he could do, which was to lift her up and hug her. "Go on back home. I'll make some calls. See if I could find someone for you. Okay?" He turned her around and with a gentle push, sent her on her way. Marina turned up right then about her husband, who had taken ill with some strange ailment. She explained to him what was happening.

"Don't you worry. We'll make it right. Or at least try. Maybe it's not what you think. Isn't it possible that your husband caught some bacteria or germ from the truck and this is a delayed reaction?"

"No. I'm sure it is the handkerchief."

"Let's not rule out anything, okay? Go get ready and I'll come around with the car and we'll go see the doctor."

"The health office is closed now. And we don't have money for a private doctor."

"It's on me. We'll take him to my doctor."

Clothilde scratched her head, frowning at her husband. What on earth has gotten into him? He was always so cold to anyone's problems, which was the main reason she married him and stayed with him all these years. Suddenly he's all compassionate and caring. He's even offered to take the neighbors to his doctor and foot the bill. Clothilde slowly walked up to her front door and stood there looking in the direction of Mario and Marina's house after her husband drove off. He didn't even bathe and change clothes. He just slipped on his shoes, grabbed the car keys, and left. Maybe the handkerchief is polluting his mind too.

The doctor prescribed some antibiotics to be applied on the affected areas twice per day. Marina didn't appear to have any faith in the medicine, insisting that medical doctors could only help when the problem is scientific, whereas her husband's problem was otherwise.

She prayed and sang hymns all the way from the doctor's office to her house. When she stopped singing, John asked her about the strange language. She answered, "Latin. We were told that prayers prayed in Latin is most powerful. So whenever we encounter an insurmountable problem, we use Latin."

John, with his strict Catholic upbringing, knew enough Latin to recognize it, even if it's pronounced incorrectly. And that was no Latin. He was wondering whether he was too quick in offering his help when he heard, "Stop it! Don't you dare do that" coming from the Headley's house. He turned in time to see Mike and Tommy rushing out from their house. Marina, in the midst of helping her husband out of the car, dropped him. He was deteriorating so rapidly that by this time, he was incapacitated and as light as a feather.

"Oh my goodness. What now?" Marina exclaimed as she watched the two boys run pell-mell up the street with a cloud of blue smoke following them.

"Mr. John, what's happening? Things were fine when I woke this morning. Then I fell and hurt nothing but my pride and dignity. All because Miss Sexy was passing in the road at the time. Then a gift outside the front door, which that stupid Mario brought into the house. Then, Mr. John, it's been steadily going downhill. Look at my husband. He's like a head of cabbage. Now there's blue smoke following the Headley boys. What's happening, Mr. John?"

"Either a spiritual force or an alien force is at work here. That's all I can say, Marina. I don't know," said Mr. John.

"What's the difference?"

"Well, now, I should say that spiritual would be like, uh…let's say, the devil at work, or some demon or entity, I think. And alien would be beings from outer space."

"And you think the devils, etc., and the beings from outer space have nothing better to do than harass us here in these backwoods? Heck, Mr. John, all the lights go out by ten o'clock!"

"Well, what do you think? Look at your husband! He's just lying there on the ground. Can't move an inch. And he was fine until he touched that gift. Do you know what it was?"

"No, I told him to get rid of it. I assumed he did."

"He didn't. It was the white handkerchief that was in the deceased shirt pocket. Mike and Tommy stole it and placed it on your doorstep."

Marina put her fist in her mouth to stifle the scream that was threatening to escape. "What?" she whispered. "So it's the ghost of Mr. Lawrence who's hurting my husband?"

Marina took a long hard look at Mario still there on the ground beside them.

"Please help me get him into the house. Mr. Lawrence was bedridden for a few months before he passed away, am I right?"

"Yes. And there was all this scratching too. I remember hearing the nurses say they were compelled to tie his hands for fear of him scratching away his flesh," Mr. John informed her.

"Just like Mario. So this is what it's all about. Now that I know what I'm dealing with, I know what to do. No one messes with my husband and gets away with it. I'll fix them good and proper."

After ensuring that Mario and Marina were settled in, Mr. John went to the Headleys', where he demanded to see the boys. He thought they were back home, but they weren't. He instead had a chat with their mother.

"Do you know who told them about the handkerchief, what to do with it, and what would happen?" Mr. John could be quite stern when necessary.

"No. I don't."

"Don't you lie to me now."

"I'm telling you the truth. I don't know. I don't even know where they are now. They ran out screaming, 'Don't you dare,' and there was that blue smoke following them. They did tell me about the white handkerchief, but not in detail. I called Mrs. Mackenzie right away. You know the rest. The police only just drove away with the body." Mrs. Headley was fidgeting so much that what she was saying couldn't be the whole truth.

"Okay. I'll have to see what can be done."

"Do you know of anyone who could fix this situation?"

"Yes. Me," replied Mr. John and left with a determination in his step that none had ever seen or heard before. Mrs. Headley stared after him with her mouth hanging open. Mr. John was thought of as a henpecked husband who had a low level of intelligence. You never know with some people.

He returned with Mike and Tommy in tow. "Now you're going to tell your mother what you told me," he said to them after sitting them down.

"Start," Mr. John said.

"We overheard Miss Clothilde talking with someone behind the school."

They were explaining when Mrs. Headley interjected, "What is this, Mr. John? You're asking them to—"

"Wait and listen. We didn't see who she was talking to. We didn't hear them either. But she said if someone should take the handkerchief form the pocket of a dead man in his coffin and wipe his face with it, he'd become possessed and really do some terrible things."

"Okay, boys, that's enough. Now you know who. Go to your room," he said to them. Mrs. Headley was dumbfounded. "What does all this mean?"

"It was you who said all those hurtful things against that girl in school, right?"

"What are you talking about?"

"You claimed that Chloe was having an affair with the shopkeeper. A man old enough be her father. And you passed it on to Clothilde. You never came to her defence when she was accused of slander. And poor thing, she couldn't prove her innocence. No one would believe her over the daughter of the school principal. After all these years, you still never owned up."

"We were kids. Just kids. I'm sorry."

"Maybe so. But you are all grown up now. And what happened then has made my wife what she is now."

"But how did you know?"

"I didn't. Not until I saw that blue smoke following the boys. My father was a seer man. A medicine man, if you will."

"You mean he sees things like spirit and stuff?"

"Yes. He left when I was still a child. But that power is inherited. It can't be taught. So I called up the smoke and had a chat. Found the boys and brought them back. What you and this entire community did to one of your own was unforgivable and inexcusable."

"So this is revenge? But my children weren't even born then. They had nothing to do with this! Will they be all right?"

"I don't know. But I can tell you this. It is not the spirit of Mr. Lawrence. That handkerchief did not belong to him. The owner is who killed Mrs. Mackenzie. My wife intended one thing, but something else happened. And what she said was true. You'll need someone really powerful to exorcise the community. Because it will torment everyone. Me? I am taking my wife away from here."

"You can't leave us like this!"

"I can, and I will. We've been married and living here all these years and you, and I do mean you yourself, have never ever stretched a hand out to her. Even knowing that you are solely responsible for her predicament. No. No, no, no. I have no sympathy for you. But I will give you a clue. It is not an entity. It is not a devil. It is a demon you are dealing with. May God have mercy on your souls. Goodbye." Mr. John tipped his hat and was gone.

In a quandary and not knowing which way to turn, Mrs. Headley headed on over to Marina and Mario's.

"Marina?" she shouted even before getting to the gate.

"Come in. Door's open."

Maria was mixing a concoction of some foul-smelling stuff in an old galvanized bucket in the kitchen. Something else was bubbling on the stove.

"Yuck! What's that smell?" She screwed her face. "Something died in here?"

"Didn't you hear? Something came back from the cemetery and is about to torment all of us. I am going to do my utmost to defend and protect my family. Now it's all man jack for himself. Look at my husband, Mrs. Headley. This morning he was a healthy, happy-go-lucky energetic individual. Now he's a fumbling idiot, can't do a thing for himself. When he pees himself, it stinks to high heaven."

"But what exactly are you doing? That smell alone will get rid of us before getting rid of whatever it is you want gone." Mrs. Headley covered her nose while trying to talk.

"What's that noise?" Marina asked.

"That would be Mr. John and his wife moving out," Mrs. Headley answered. Something in her voice told Marina not all was well.

"Out with it," she said without missing a turn of the pot.

"He said it's a demon come to torment us all, so he's taking his wife to safety," she answered timidly with head bowed, not looking at Marina.

"What does that mean? I know he went after the smoke that was following your boys. It's you who's responsible for all this!" It suddenly dawned on Marina what exactly was going on. "You did some harm to someone and now we all have to suffer for it? Oh no! I thought it was the spirit of Mr. Lawrence sent by Clothilde. But no. It's more than that. It is something to do with you. What is it?"

Mrs. Headley had no choice but to recount the entire story from school days. She managed to do so without shedding a tear. "And he's right, Marina. May God have mercy on our souls. Because there's no one to help us. Our parish priest is away on retreat for one month. Mrs. Mackenzie is dead. My boys, who were used, are scared all the time. They are locked up in their room afraid to come out. I am so sorry for that incident during our school days."

"Yes, we all hurt, Clothilde. Well, now we all have to take our punishment."

A shrieking sound suddenly pierced the air, and looking at each other, they asked with one voice, "What is that?"

The blue smoke appeared in the kitchen and slowly formed into a giant of a monster with two beautifully shaped horns and a long tail like that of a crocodile or an alligator. From its jaw dripped thick heavy mucus, and its hands, which were reaching for them, had long tapered fingernails akin to knives. They screamed. The last sound they ever made.

THE MUTANT ZOMBIE

Jules sneaked into the warehouse in the early morning hours, sure no one was about to witness his act of lawlessness. He gathered up the pitchfork and shovel and went to the cemetery, intent on getting his father out of the cold earth where they installed him. Jules was sure his father couldn't breathe down there, and he had to do something. In tears, he slowly trekked to the area where he thought they'd buried his loving father.

Three feet down, he saw a hand, but his father was in a box, he was sure of it. What happened to it? Too late he realized his mistake. This was the wrong cemetery.

He tried to cover it back, but the hand came to life, followed by the rest of the body, which was in an advanced state of decomposition. Jules watched motionless as the thing arose, all six feet of him, and rumbling, he shook off dirt along with bits of flesh from its body. Jules steered clear of the falling bits of stink. He tried to crawl away but was grabbed by the scruff of the neck and lifted to eye level of the beast. Jules couldn't cry. He couldn't scream. But he could shut his eyes, and that he did.

He got the salt from his pocket and threw it into the eyes of the thing. It was of no use. It did work on other beasts but not this one. He drove a knife through the chest, again nothing. Time to panic, he wiggled to get free, but to no avail. He saw the mouth opening and struggled to keep his head from its mouth, and finally succeeding, he dropped to the earth, grabbing bits of flesh on the way down.

He scrambled away, tripping on tree roots and moving earth. He stopped to survey the location and saw the earth all around him moving. With the rising of the sun, he could now see clearly, and the dead was coming up out of their final resting place. Looking around, he saw the sign, which was covered with some vines and barely noticeable, "Home of the Zombies. Stay Out." There was the fence with yellow string tied all the way across. He remembered cutting it to enter. Then he remembered the priest with the long orange gown about a year ago, who performed some strange ritual and instructed that the string must never be broken. Now he knows why. The zombies, who were all under heavy manners, were now free to roam and eat. He felt, rather than saw, the group of them coming at him, hands outstretched, hungry and closing in for the kill.

He made a dash for the wide-open space where he could run freely, because the zombies were slow and rigid. He was sure he'd escape them when he fell and hit his head on a boulder. When he came to, the zombies were just bending over him. He barely managed to escape those teeth that refuse to fall off like flesh, by rolling like a ball. He shinnied up the lone coconut tree and watched them tumble over each other just as the town was waking up. Traffic was coming along, and people were going to work. The result of his actions was now hitting him.

Their attention drawn to the sounds of traffic emanating from the town, the zombies turned in that direction. Jules used this moment to climb down and head back to the zombie home for a piece of the yellow thread. He tied a piece around his waist and headed toward the crowd, who were scampering and screaming, trying to get away from the zombies. They appeared to be multiplying, because there is no way he could be responsible for all that mayhem.

He crawled through someone's backdoor and explained to them the meaning of the yellow thread.

"I'll try anything. I don't want to be a zombie," said Mr. Johnson, the head of the household.

He, his wife, and two grown sons tied it directly on to their bodies, and with that new confidence, they grabbed whatever length of wood or pipeline they could lay their hands on and went to meet the enemy head on. They were furious at having their daily routine so rudely interrupted.

After a few minutes of slashing and swiping at the zombies, one of the sons said, "Jules, what exactly is this thread supposed to do?"

"Well, it kept them in the ground for a few years," Jules answered.

"Aargh!" the man screamed. "It doesn't work!"

Jules paused for a moment to look at the man's arm, and he was grabbed from behind. He could feel his flesh being chewed off. He turned while slashing with all the strength he could muster. He could feel the initial pain already numbing and his movements becoming awkward and slow. He was becoming a zombie. But still he fought on. He would not give up the fight until he was fully turned.

He saw the priest, still wearing the long orange gown, to the far side of the commotion. In his hand, he held a string of beads that he was spinning in the air. Jules walked toward the priest, and the zombies followed him. He found his mind to be clearer and sharper than it's ever been. His footsteps also were no longer slow. All those with the yellow string did turn into zombies after being bitten, but then turned again or grew into something undefined.

There was something akin to recognition mixed with terror on the face of the priest.

Jules felt an intense hatred building up from within, which he told himself should not be if he was a zombie. He touched his back, where he was bitten, and felt it wet and slimy. He looked at his hands and saw a green slimy stuff, unlike the black decaying fluid that came from the original zombies.

He questioned the priest about this phenomenon. There were too many inconsistencies. He also had the power of speech.

The priest explained that something went terribly wrong when Jules cut the string and accidentally cut his hand, thereby causing a drop of blood to awaken the spirit within the said string. That spirit had never tasted blood and found he liked it, resulting in the creation of a rebel. "He enticed the zombies to ensure they bit you, making you a new kind. A mutant, if you will."

Jules fully realized what all this meant. He was a zombie with all the faculties intact, including intelligence and the need for revenge. But worst of all is he cannot die. Now he understood the horrifying fear in the eyes of the priest, who never stopped spinning those confounded beads.

Too late the priest took to his heels, and the horde of zombies were upon him at the signal from their leader, Jules.

THE VEIL OF SAHARA

Sahara sat at her desk, elbows resting, chin in her hands, propping sorrow. Her long straight black hair, stringy and in a bunch, just as sad and in sympathy with their owner, who wasn't up to washing or grooming it. Her colleagues at their desks paid her no mind, not even a greeting. She was nonexistent as far as they were concerned.

Sahara never did notice the head of the department was paying close attention to her. Every day for the past two weeks. But she did notice the strikingly handsome man who visited the office occasionally. Those visits became more frequent as she presumed he got accustomed to the stares from the employees. They did so with unabashed curiosity. On this day, impeccably dressed in a black suit with a white Nehru collar that accentuated his high cheekbones and beak-like nose, he left an indelible mark on the heart of Sahara. His unusually pale skin reminded her of her own parents, who never ventured out during the daytime.

He gently closed the door to Melvina's office, and as inconspicuous as she was, Sahara walked past the door hoping for a snippet of conversation, just to hear the intonation of that romantic accent in his voice.

"I think you are right, Melvina. Sahara is a perfect candidate." She stood transfixed at the mention of her name. She clutched her chest, warm blood rising to her face and her breath coming fast and furious. A smile broke through as she visualized his strong arms holding her closely. A sound of ecstasy involuntarily escaped her lips, and shocked beyond belief, she ran to the bathroom. She didn't notice that as usual, no one was paying any attention to her. Not so Melvina and her companion. A smile escaped their lips simultaneously.

"See what I mean?" said Melvina.

"Yes. She's ripe and ready. How about this weekend? Can you get her to attend?" Hennessey was firm.

"I'll do better. I'll bring her around. You have everything ready. This should be a blast." Melvina was only too willing to do as asked.

Sahara went to her priest that evening to confess the sin of thought, if not in word and deed. She religiously attended the Sunday services and confession once per month, but after the sinful thoughts involving Melvina's visitor, she decided it would be better to go now and ensure her salvation and her seat in heaven.

Shocked and astonished at the invitation from Melvina to, as she said, a get-together in an upscale part of town with some high-profile people, she gladly accepted. If only to meet and have a chat with that handsome man. Definitely out of her league, but since she doesn't fit in anywhere, maybe this will be different. She complained she didn't have the kind of clothes for that gathering, but Melvina brushed that aside and explained, "No one does, dear. So we have outfits for all shapes and sizes. Don't worry. I'll pick you up at, say, nine o'clock? We'll get you there and outfitted. You'll be fine, you'll look great, and you'll have a wonderful time."

She gently squeezed Sahara's arm, resulting in an unexplainable tingle throughout her body. She surmised that it was because of the cold. The room was unusually cold today.

Melvina, punctual as ever, knocked on her door promptly at nine, dressed in the smart business suit she wears to the office. Understanding that Sahara would be feeling underdressed, Melvina put her at ease on the way to her car.

"You'll be fine, Sahara. Don't worry so. If it will make you feel any better, we'll go through the back entrance, okay?"

"Thank you." She twisted her hair around her fingers in a rigidly nervous state.

"You'll fit in quite nicely. You've got the discipline and the deportment, along with good manners. You should never ever allow others to make you feel less than you are."

"I understand," Sahara answered meekly.

"I don't think you do, Sahara," Melvina replied, causing Sahara to feel even more despondent.

"Sorry. I don't think that came out quite right. What I mean is, you're not aware of the power you possess. That inner ability to sway others to your way of thinking and doing what you want without uttering a word. I have seen it and understand it."

"You have?" Sahara hung on every word uttered. She'd heard but never listened to Melvina before now. Her words were pronounced with a sharp edge but not quite harsh. They dripped with austerity but still sweet and mellow to Sahara's inner self. Something with which she was unaware till now.

"Believe me, yes. And so has my friend Hennessey. You've seen him occasionally coming to visit me. He's not a business acquaintance but an old friend. A very old friend. And a very wise man. He's seen it too. As a matter of fact, he's the one who insisted that I bring you along tonight."

Sahara turned away as she felt the blood rushing to her face. She didn't see Melvina licking her lips as she smelt the rush of fresh blood.

As she turned the car into the massive driveway, dimly lit with colorful bulbs beneath the hedge, Sahara caught her breath. *What kind of place is this?* she silently asked herself.

"This is amazing, Melvina. I've never seen anything like it."

"Actually, you have. You just don't remember."

· They entered an elevator straight out of the car after Melvina handed the keys to who Sahara thought was a valet. She'd read of them in books, though she never had the privilege of encountering one in real life. His mechanical movements had her wondering whether he was human. The elevator went down a few flights, and asking Melvina about it, she was told, "Our clientele is very exclusive and private. They avoid publicity, hence the reason for the club being a few miles underground. It's not easily accessible to anyone who is not a member."

"Yet you invite me? Me?" And she pointed a finger at herself in consternation.

Melvina gently rubbed her arm and smiling, said, "I told you. You are special. Before the night is over, you will see for yourself. Come on. This way." Sahara was led through a door marked simply 'Dish,' to the left of a long corridor with very little lighting. Music could be heard coming from behind a door on the opposite side. After passing a few more doors, they entered what looked like a dress shop with rows and rows of all kinds of dresses. Formal, evening, party, there was even beach wear and other stuff that could be waitress uniforms. Sahara knew better than to ask any question that might sound rude and impertinent or out of place. She didn't want to cross the line.

"Let's see what suits you. First, you dress for introductions, then for dancing and lastly for mingling," Melvina explained to her while searching for appropriate outfits.

"Three outfits for one evening?" Sahara said, astonished. *What kind of get-together is this?* she silently questioned herself. However, she changed into the gown that was chosen for her. A white floor-length, off-the-shoulder dress with a slit reaching up to her thighs. It was also quite see-through. Even though she was a bit uncomfortable at the indecency of it, she smiled. Time to be rebellious. At twenty-five, she hadn't done a thing worthwhile or radical in her life. Now's the time to start. After all it's being handed to her on a platter. She might as well enjoy it to the fullest. Melvina called in the resident makeup artist, and when done, Sahara was unrecognizable but exceedingly beautiful. She admired herself so much that she found a new self-confidence and walked into the main hall to be introduced with her head held high. Not too many people, she guessed just about twenty or so. She noticed that they all had straight black hair, even the men, reaching the middle of their back. All had different complexions, and they all wore the same white gown. The men were dressed in white shirts and white pants, After the introductions, with Hennessy being the last, they went on to change for the dance.

Sahara could feel that rush again on seeing him, but the touch was out of this world. She had no words to describe that feeling, but no, nothing like that was allowed to happen. Apparently

Melvina sensed it and pulled her away, guiding her to the changing room again.

"Sit here for a bit. I think it's a bit much for you to handle all at once. Sorry. Maybe I should have taken it a bit slower. No matter. We'll manage, and you'll enjoy it all."

"You know. I'm sorry." Sahara tried to explain away her feelings, to no avail. Melvina brushed her off like swatting a fly.

"You worry too much, Sahara. Keep your cool. We're all one in here. Come take a peak."

Sahara was shocked beyond words at the sight before her eyes.

"See what I mean? We share and share alike. And no, Hennessey is not there. He's waiting for you. Understand? You have no need to worry. You belong to him, and he belongs to you."

"I don't understand."

"I know you don't. But wait a little longer. Your appointed time is fast approaching. Sit here and compose yourself. I'll be back in a minute."

Sahara was now totally sure that hell will be her final resting place. These thoughts and sights and feelings can't be healthy for one's soul. She let out a sigh that couldn't by any stretch of the imagination be classified as dejection or rejection. It was a sigh of intense longing, of unequalled joy, unparallel happiness to be here where she belonged. She heard voices behind the door. Melvina's. And yes. Hennessey's. She strained her ears to hear the conversation. They were talking about her. What about her that had them so interested in her. She distinctly heard a line, as though they'd just come to a conclusion or agreement on something.

"She just paused at the door again. There is no doubt that she is our leader." Hennessey was emphatic in his declaration.

"I agree with you there. But what exactly does it all mean?" Melvina, however, had some kind of growl in her voice. It was no longer sweet. "What does 'leader' mean? We've been fine for some three centuries or so. We grow our own food…"

"Exactly, Melvina. She paused at the door to the farm. Why? Did you ask yourself that?"

"Yes. She was daydreaming about having it on with you. And only you."

"No, no, no, Melvina. I think you're losing it. Think, you block-head!" shouted Hennessey in exasperation, hands flailing in the air around his head.

Melvina face turned a glowing red, so furious was she, and with her fingernails lengthening and twisting, she levitated, with her hair curling like a corkscrew, and attacked Hennessey, who did not meta-morphose but kept his balance and good sense, sidestepped, and braked all her onslaughts. She got so mad at his insistence not to fight back that she attempted to use her fangs on him, which was against the rules. He let her, whereby she lost all her vampire pow-ers. She gazed up at him as she slowly sank to the floor, her strength giving way to total weakness and apathy. Hennessey lifted her bodily and laid her on a settee.

"Told you that your envious nature would ruin you. Sahara is the one we've been waiting for."

"What are you talking about? Who is Sahara?"

"She's our leader, Melvina. And now all you're good for is to ensure the farm is kept full and clean. Such a waste. Oh well, we did have some good times."

He let out a blood-curdling yell that was the cue to come and get fresh new meat. Then Sahara, oblivious to all this, walked through the door that was actually drawing her in.

There she saw what is called the farm. A large room separated into compartments with humans, then teenagers, and so on accord-ing to their age groups. She was amazed at the texture of their skin, which was quite clear and clean. No blemishes whatsoever. She also noticed a cupboard with foodstuffs that was grown only by light. None of them had the power of speech. Hennessey approached her from behind.

"I see you've found the source of our food supply. What do you think?" he inquired.

"I understand now what Melvina was hinting at. I'm responsi-ble for this somehow?"

"Yes. I initially thought that you were a direct descendant of the one who created this project. But no, I was wrong. You are the one who actually created it. I don't know how you come to be here. I just know that it's you."

"Yes. And you really are mine. So how about we get the ball rolling? It's been so long. Tell me why the farm?" Sahara asked

"You deduced that if our food is pure and clean, we'd go on that much longer because there'd be no need to go outside for the villagers, who'd become adept at hunting and killing us. Also, our fangs would be nice and sharp and attractive."

"Nice and attractive? What does that mean?" she questioned

"Well, the authorities have messed with agriculture so much that when we drink the blood of those that eat that kind of food, it affects our teeth and our minds and makes us careless. Our numbers were dwindling so much that we were forced to retreat underground." he explained in detail.

"You came up with the idea of the human farm." He continued, "After all, we always need. And what better way to make a lot of it? We have a ready-made clientele who'd always keep the secret."

Hennessey growled at the sound of the urn as it fell from the topmost shelf. They all froze, unable to move. He sprang from his position with Sahara and flew to the closest one and bit him so harsh that his head came off. Simultaneously Sahara reached for the closest without moving from her spot. Her hands stretched like elastic, and she squeezed until he was destroyed. But then she called a halt, and Hennessey stopped in the midst of drinking his food and shoved away his prey, who stayed where he fell.

"It's time to move above ground, my love. I'll take my rightful place in Melvina's chair. I've got a bone to pick with all those who work in that department," stated Sahara.

"And you'll enjoy that. But from where will we function?" Hennessey countered.

"Our base will be, uh, let's see...somewhere up north?"

"Yes, I hear the climate is salubrious." And he laughed, mocking those who use such words.

"The farm will stay here. We'll appoint a committee to oversee such matters. You'll take care of that." Sahara was exercising her authority with no effort whatsoever.

"The women from your department could fill in there," Hennessey offered.

"You're right. They won't be missed. Okay, that's settled. I think I'm home," she ended. "Let's celebrate."

"Gladly. Sahara's veil has been lifted. Welcome home," said Hennessey.

A DEAL WITH THE DEVIL

S amson put the sleeping pill in his wife's drink, ensuring a full night's sleep. Making sure the house was secured, he gathered the bag that he'd already packed and feeling his heart pounding in his chest, walked out the door into the darkness.

At the riverbank, he stripped naked, wrapped the clean white towel around his neck, as per instructions, and stood quite still. Facing the river, eyes closed, breath coming in short spurts, he waited for the terrifying sounds.

There must not be any signs of fear, he was told, or he'll be rejected.

Heart thumping, he concentrated on what his best friend, Selwyn, had said to him, should he pass the initiation process and get accepted.

"Keep your mind on the prize. A golden pot that will never run out of money."

And the rules.

"Keep your hands flat against your legs. A clenched fist is a sign of fear."

"I am not a coward, man," he'd replied. "And all I have to do is stand at the riverbank with my eyes closed?"

"At three in the morning. The hour is crucial to the outcome." Selwyn was quite adamant about this point.

The devil's hour now at hand, he wanted to pray, but knew he shouldn't. Even though he was in the heart of the forest, he knew for a fact that there were no animals like lion and tiger in this part of the world, so he was unprepared for the sounds of their roaring. He was warned that some of the sounds would be of dangerous animals.

When he heard the sounds of lions roaring and snakes hissing very close to him, he nearly peed himself but remembered Selwyn had said, "Don't you dare pee yourself. The big man doesn't like nastiness." Something was now licking his face, and it was putrid and slimy. Samson was beside himself with fear, but successful in not showing an inkling of it. He desperately needed all that money.

Suddenly he heard this gravelly voice close to his ear whispering loudly, if that's at all possible, to bend over and touch his toes. Thinking of the reward, he did as he was instructed.

The towel touched the ground, and there was some foul-smelling liquid poured all over him, even as the towel seemed to come alive and snaked itself around him, hissing all the while. To stave off the fear, Samson visualized all the cars he'd have in his garage and passed the test with flying colors.

The gravelly voice said, "Done."

He wasn't sure what to do, but he opened his eyes, and he was not at the river but on a highway, which was strange because in this part of the country, there were no roads, per se, but only tracks.

Disoriented, he looked down at himself and found he was dressed in a suit, complete with shoes and a homburg hat. He had no idea of the time, but out of habit, he looked at his wrist, and there was a watch. Even though it was dark, he could see a bit from the light of the sky. It was one o'clock.

He heard the galloping of horses, but there were none in sight. Then there were the sounds of donkeys braying, dogs barking, cows mooing, but no animals could be seen. No human beings either. Strangely enough, he felt no fear. He thought he now had nerves of steel. He was so excited in his newfound persona that he punched the air, laughing uproariously, and yelled to the world, "I don't need you!"

"Who don't you need, honey?"

Samson swiveled on his heel and spun around to face the owner of the voice. It couldn't be his wife. He'd fed her enough pills to last at least eight hours.

"Becca? What are you doing here?" he inquired with the hint of a mischievous grin.

"You left the house three years ago, sweetheart. So naturally, I sent out scouts to find you," Becca explained with her most charming smile.

"You're mistaken, Becca. I left a few hours ago. Left you sound asleep," Samson answered with his charming smile.

"You went to make a deal with the devil." That couldn't be his Becca. That voice was way too gruff. "You wanted easy money with benefits. This is it." Then spreading her arms to encompass all the land for miles around with no vegetation continued. "Look around you. You're in charge of all this land and all who should drop in."

Samson stood transfixed, staring at her with his mouth open and eyes as wide as saucers.

A loud plop punctuated the atmosphere, and looking around, Samson saw two men with blood that apparently just stopped flowing from a deep gash on their throats. They were quite filthy, and the violence in their eyes was quite unnerving.

"I'm your guide through this journey upon which you chose to embark." And Becca laughed, showing jagged teeth while her face metamorphosed into something so hideous and abominable all the fear he'd experienced from his youth up came flooding back.

He was speechless as Becca came toward him with breath so foul he bent over to vomit, but nothing came out. He experienced an unknown feeling of nothingness whereby he should have felt a bit of shock or surprise, but nothing was there.

Becca stood watching him up close, so close he should feel her breath on him but again nothing. So what was that smell a minute ago? His mind in a whirl, he asked for an explanation.

"You won't have to work like you understand work, Samson. This is it from here on. Every so often, a few souls would drop in. Like those two. They are definitely not for upstairs and not quite ready for downstairs. Your job is to prepare them for downstairs. Succeed and you'll be the new recruiter, walking in Selwyn's shoes. Your partner will be, uh, uh…who'll be his partner?" Her head spun to the side as she questioned Selwyn, who'd just appeared out of nowhere.

"Oh, I don't know. Does it matter?" he answered, and they laughed in that ugly gravelly voice which brought Samson to his senses.

He'd momentarily forgotten the prayers he'd learned in childhood, but they now came flooding back. He shouted prayers like he never did before. A tremendous roar of thunder broke through the skies with flashes of lightning in its wake. The roars of the weird animals turned to screams, and they were just as scary and revolting as previously.

Selwyn, pulled from behind as if by a lasso and spinning in the air, landed plump on his face and was a bit squashed as he tried to lift up himself. He came shuffling from the sides of the highway, his face grimacing and his fingers elongated, with pus oozing where the fingernails should be.

"Selwyn? What's going on?" Samson questioned his friend, gazing at him incredulously.

"Sorry, friend. But I needed my stripes and could only get them by recruiting one who is willing and want to get something for nothing. I wanted to live in the two worlds with the love of my life, Becca."

"You tricked me?"

"Well, yeah. Guess so. But I forgot you are the son of a priest."

Both Selwyn and Becca simultaneously clapped their hands, and Samson felt himself being propelled at increasing speed through the air filled with indescribable sights and sounds that definitely weren't of this world. He fell hard on stones, and when he was able to focus, he found he was on the same riverbank, but was blind in one eye and missing a leg, and the shiny and new golden goblet sitting there.

CURSED BY THE CHURCH

There she was again, with a baby in her arms. A cute little thing just a few months old, so new and pale, with her hair crowning her face. She was quiet, too quiet. I first noticed them during the church service a few weeks ago.

Today I glanced at the members of the congregation, but nobody paid any attention to her. She just stood there on the doorstep outside the church, looking in. I wondered, *Why didn't she come in?* She was dressed in the same long white gown, and likewise the baby in the same white dress. Obviously she is mother to baby, sad and forlorn. She was tall and elegant but so pale, with a head scarf and no makeup.

This day I will talk to her, maybe start a conversation. She is probably in need of some kind of help. And since I have no commitments, I could spare a few moments to help a fellow human being. The service over, I made my way to where she was, only to find her gone. I questioned the members about her identity and whereabouts, but none could say. They all shook their heads with a frown that said, what are you talking about?

Next Sunday there she was again. This time, I went straight to her without going into the church. She took a step back and held the baby even tighter, her face devoid of emotion. I turned to the altar to genuflect, but when I turned back, she was gone. I searched all around the church and eventually found her a little way up the street.

"There you are. I thought you'd gone. Is the baby all right?" I asked with some degree of concern.

Her lips moved, but no words could come out.

"Yes." That monosyllable exited with such relief that the silence that ensued was loud enough to be noticeable.

"I've seen you just outside the church a few times. You never enter. Is there a reason?" When she didn't answer, I continued, "Do you live around here? Where is your family?" When she still didn't answer, I told her that I was late for an appointment and left.

I was disappointed at the silent rebuff, so much as to feel dejected. I wanted to lash out at someone, anyone. There was absolutely no plausible reason why I should feel this way, but I did. It's not like I was appointed her savior, mentor, or whatever. For no earthly reason, she rejected the hand I stretched out to her, and in so doing, she rejected me. I'm going to approach her again. Yes, I will. Especially as I now realize that it is for me and not her. The concern that I feel has nothing to do with her or her baby; it is for me.

My life was empty with no one to care for, no one to care for me. If I am late getting home, there's no one to worry. None to file a missing person's report. If I miss a day's work, they'll just call the agency for a replacement. So this is why I must get a response from this person. There's a void in my life that must be filled.

Maybe it was my determination or confidence in realizing the reason I was approaching this person, but she was quite friendly the next church day.

"Hello," I greeted her. "Allow me to introduce myself. I am Marcia. I live up the street, moved into Mr. Hudson's house a few months ago. I live alone and work at the supermarket. I'm heading to the botanical gardens for a lonely picnic. Would you like to come along?" I rambled on and was surprised at the hint of a smile. She walked with me, not uttering one single word. I chose a spot with the president's house in our line of vision and the guards could be seen patrolling the grounds.

She paid no attention to the scenery, choosing rather to keep her gaze fixed on my face. I didn't bother to ask her name but kept up a steady monologue, thankful for some company, even if silent.

But there was this uncanny feeling in the pit of my stomach that seemed to be growing more intense so that it could no longer be ignored. Why does she not speak? Neither does she eat. The baby also hasn't uttered a sound. Is it dumb? But it is not moving.

"How would you like to stay with me for a few days?" I must have been out of my mind, as I heard myself make the offer, but I was in dire need of some company. Someone to care for, on whom to spend some money. I needed a purpose. This case presented itself, and I'll be damned if I let it pass. She responded with the hint of a smile, and before she could vanish from sight, I grabbed the baby, and we were in my small but neat two-bedroom apartment. I got out some clothes for her so she could change from that gown she'd been wearing for weeks on end.

A few days later, she opened up and started talking. I was happy that she did, and though it was all muddled at first, I eventually understood her speech. The words were so difficult that I thought English must not be her first language. She left me with the baby more and more.

"Didn't she eat today?" I asked when I saw all the bottles still in the fridge, unused.

"She's full. Don't drink much," she said.

"Did you nurse her?" I asked.

"Yes," she answered.

"Do you smell something strange? Like burning wood?"

No." Her one-word answers was still the extent of conversations with her. But no matter, I was happy to be able to spend money on someone other than myself.

"It's been there for the past few days. Mild at first, but it's more pronounced now. Maybe someone's burning land close by. Nothing to worry about, I hope," I finally said.

"No."

"How about a walk? Might be good for the baby. She does sleep a lot, doesn't she? I've never seen her awake," I remarked.

"Yes. Hold the baby with one hand and take my hand with the other," she told me, quite clearly now. And surprising as the request was, I did as she asked without question and was immediately transported to an unrecognizable location.

The first words out of her mouth shocked me out of my wits.

"This is where we died." She said it. I know she did. I heard her say it. But I couldn't believe it.

"Is this some kind of a joke? If so, I don't find it funny," I said to her as I tried to hand the baby to her.

"No." She held up both hands, palms facing me. "You hold her. She's now yours."

"What?" I'm sure I heard wrong. "What do you mean by that? I only offered to help you a bit, not take your baby."

"Oh, she'll be no trouble at all. All you have to do is hold her. Like you're doing now."

That scent of wood burning was so strong now that it was getting most uncomfortable. It was stifling and stinging my nostrils at the same time. I had a bout of sneezing. When I suddenly glanced at her, the expression on her face was so hateful and grotesque that I froze. But only for a second or two. I quickly regained my composure and smiled. I had no idea what I was dealing with.

"It is your fault that I have to carry a baby throughout all eternity. I didn't ask for this. I don't want this. And I absolutely refuse it."

Her voice grew gravelly and terrible. I raised my eyes toward the sky, expecting to see the clouds rolling over each other, but it wasn't so. The vast expanse of sky was dark. Darker than it's ever been. I turned again, seeking some semblance of sanity lurking in the corners or behind a tree or even swinging on a branch, but no, nobody and no one to help me.

"Let me see if I understand this. You are not of this world."

"I am, but I am not."

"What does that mean exactly?"

Her voice had reverted to normal again, and that I could handle.

"I had a heart condition which necessitated a transplant. My good fortune provided a donor instantly. By that, I mean the very same day. Like she was waiting for me. The church disagreed with me accepting the heart of another. I was told to recognize when my life has come to an end and accept it. But I could not do that. All I ever wanted was someone to call me 'Mommy.' And I did not have that as yet. So I went against the church and accepted the transplant. Two years later, I gave birth to a baby girl. The church refused to baptize her. I was devastated. So one day while driving through the rain, with the road slippery and my eyes full of tears, I missed the caution tape and crashed. My baby and I died instantly."

"I'm so sorry," I said and meant it.

"The church refused me the last rites and condemned me to walk throughout all eternity with the baby whom I've come to despise."

"But what does all that have to do with me?"

"There was a window of opportunity for release left open. If and whenever someone would pity me and offer a hand, I could hand over the baby to that person and I'll have my freedom. I still have to walk the earth, but without the baby. And you're it," she concluded and promptly vanished, leaving me with the baby, who had stuck to me like glue. I couldn't move her, put her down, or even change hands. She became part of my body.

I went home to my cold apartment and cried and cried. I don't know for how long. But the scent of burning wood lingered on.

She made one last appearance to explain the burning wood scent. She told me that a pundit felt sorry for her and cremated her body along with the baby, consigning them both to their fate.

The landlord came to collect the rent and asked, "Why do you have your arms up like that? Like you're holding a baby?"

I didn't answer him. All I could do was cry some more.

LEGION

G ary locked the door and retrieved the box from its hiding place under the bed.

Time for a drastic change in his boring life.

"Face the east, sitting cross-legged on the floor, when you open this box," his grandfather instructed him. At eighteen, he needed all the help he could get.

"Light a white candle. Keep it from blowing out." He closed all the windows.

"Repeat these words aloud. Thirteen times. Make no mistake." He had pen and paper at the ready.

He opened the box, recited the words eleven times, and the window opened, bringing in a gush of wind that blew out the candle. He gazed at it in shock, and Chuck shouted at him, "What you doing, man? This is some kind of hoodoo?"

Gary felt a knife in his hand and slashed Chuck across the face.

"Hey! What you do that for?"

Gary stuck the knife into Chuck's belly and twisted it. He kept up the slashing and sticking until Chuck was no more.

Gary surveyed his handiwork, and satisfied, he dropped on the bed and passed out.

Incessant banging on the door woke him to see his best friend gutted, headless, and mutilated on the floor of his bedroom.

"Yeah!" he shouted, and his voice was strange to his ears.

"Time to get up!" His mother insisted on punctuality. She'd never enter his room, not since she walked in on him doing boy things when he was fourteen, so he was in the clear. He didn't remember the events of last night, but his feelings right now were nonexistent.

Calmly and without any emotion or regret or even questions, he tidied up as best he could, and remembering he'd gotten to eleven when the candle blew out, he tried again to obtain the desired result.

Through a twist of fate, the candle blew out at five. The apparition was so sudden and unexpected that it brought all feelings back with a jerk. He was scared. Too scared to move.

"Who are you?" he asked, voice shaking.

"Are you sure you want to know that?" the man thing with horns and a tail and scales where there should be skin answered.

"What are you doing here? Where did you come from? What do you want?"

"So many questions. Okay. One at a time. I'm here because you called me. I'm from another plane of existence. I want to give you what you want. Of course, it must be mine to give."

"I didn't call you."

"Yes, you did. At five. You first called my brother at eleven. I recognize his handiwork."

"Oh, I see."

"He did a great job. He's wonderful at what he does."

"So what do you have to give?"

"Look in the mirror."

Gary jumped back after the first glimpse. He peeped again and got the same reaction.

"Aw, come on. It's not all that bad."

"I'm like three hundred pounds. With a beard. I look like a gorilla. And I sound like a girl."

"Yeah, but you must admit, with your mouth closed, you're hot. Isn't that how it is said?" And the apparition promptly vanished.

That night, Gary went to the only sports bar in their neck of the woods and had a flock of girls around him. This is partly what he wanted, because he could never talk to girls. He'd freeze and be tongue-tied. With his newfound bravado, he had the nerve and the vocabulary to chat them down. But they moved away within a few minutes of listening to his squeaky voice that sounded much like a mouse. And the men laughed at him. Humiliated to the core, he went walking around the small town with its one of everything, including grocery, fabric store, school, and even a cinema, with drooping shoulders and heavy dragging footsteps.

"Get out of the way old man!" a group of teenagers taunted him.

This was too much too bear, he lashed out at them, surprising himself at the strength and fury in his arm. He could feel the muscles tensing in his face as he slammed the boys to the ground one in each hand. He did it without the strength even waning a bit.

He was fully aware of it all, but unable to control himself. With one limp body held over his head, he spotted his grandfather across the street. He stood transfixed for a moment, long enough for his grandfather to throw something unidentifiable in his direction. He dropped the body and held his stomach, grimacing in pain. Again he passed out and came to in his grandfather's run-down hut at the edge of the little town.

"Gramps?"

"You didn't follow my instructions," he said as he handed him a glass of a foul-smelling liquid. Gary knew better than to screw his face at the scent of it. He downed the liquid in one unholy gulp. It unexpectedly stayed in his stomach.

"What's that supposed to do?" he asked Gramps.

"Well, it should clear away the remnants of whatever possessed you. They don't all go away. Some of their traits are left behind. Actually this concoction was meant for the thirteenth brother. I'm not sure if or how it will work with the others. I've never met them."

"What?" Gary's eyes almost popped out of their sockets. So incredulous was he.

"My instructions were specific, Gary. You messed up."

"It wasn't my fault, Gramps. Chuck came through the window."

"It was up to you to ensure that all doors and windows were locked."

"What do I do now?" he asked his grandfather.

"Well, we shall have to wait about two days, see what happens, and move on from there," he answered, but Gary could sense the uneasiness and uncertainty in his voice.

Gary's mother did notice some strange behavioral patterns developing in her son, and she was perturbed about them. She knew about her father's abilities but steered clear of them. She was not that way inclined. But she eventually came to the conclusion that he did have something to do with what was happening to her son. She approached her father with her deductions, but he was furious and adamant that he had nothing to do with whatever was happening to Gary.

On the second day, Gary was summoned to the principal's office, where he met with the hierarchy of the school. He was a petrified, wondering what he'd done or if they'd somehow found out about his extracurricular activities.

"Have a seat, Gary," said the principal, his mustache bobbing up and down and his tie twisted as usual. "We'd like some clarifications and, of course, some explanations on these book reports you've submitted over the past two days."

"Yes? What about them?" he queried, while he pondered on the realization that the fright was only a memory of past instances when he was sent to this office. His body was quite confident. No fear whatsoever.

"Well, they're perfect. Accurate. Well researched and formulated. And that in itself is questionable. How can you move from an F student to an A+ in two days? Did you steal these reports?"

"No, sir. I did them myself, sir."

"Can you prove that?"

"Yes, sir. Would you like the proof now, sir?"

"Don't see how you can do that, but yes. Use the phone if you want."

"No, sir, something better. Give me another book, and may I use this computer here please, sir?"

"Sure. Come use this one." Two books were sourced from the library, and they watched him, goggle-eyed, as the pages turned in quick succession as he read and typed out the report in as little as thirty minutes. Gary went on to the second book while they checked and rechecked the first. He was done with the second before they were through with the first.

"This is incredible! I know I have just seen it, but I can't believe it. I can't fathom this realization, this fact, this...I am at a loss for words." That was the dean of discipline. *So they came prepared to punish me*, thought Gary.

The English teacher said, "That's impossible. There must be some trick involved somewhere." He was furious at the results because he secretly hated Gary due to an ongoing feud between the two families. It was so old the root of which has long been forgotten. All that remained was that undying hatred. Only the principal saw the drastic change in the features of the dean. And he only saw the fist tighten so much as to bleed. The dean appeared to be swelling and growing taller as the rage consumed his body. He rubbed his eyes, and when he looked again, all was well. He smiled and said to Gary, "That will be all for today. We'll let you know if anything has to be done. Thank you, Gary."

"Thank you, sir," he answered and left the room, closing the door gently behind him. He turned left at the end of the corridor and leaned against the wall. He felt the knife in his hand, and touching his face, he felt a beard and knew that Gramps's concoction worked in ways not meant to cleanse the residue of his colossal blunder a few nights previously. He grabbed the dean in a choke hold and stabbed him in the back. He felt himself moving as quick as lightning, with all his senses intact and enjoying it. The dean, though he had also metamorphosed into something ferocious, lacked the speed and agility of Gary and was soon out of the equation.

Gary met Gramps just leaving the barber almost unrecognizable because he'd shaved his head and took of all his facial hair.

"Gramps? What have you done with yourself? But you do look good. Young," Gary complimented him, albeit with a frown.

Rubbing his head, Gramps answered, "Preparation, sonny boy, preparation."

"When you call me that, something's up. Trouble with my mistake?"

"You got that right. Your mother came to see me."

"She didn't go into my room, did she?"

"She didn't say. Tell me, anything untoward happen today?"

He recounted the events of the day, including the part where he was aware of everything and felt good about it.

"That's what I was afraid of. They're stuck with you, and eventually they'll come for me. They like their freedom. As it is, they are no longer free to roam and jump on the backs of anybody, and they blame me."

"But they can't have been free if they were locked up in a box."

"It goes further than that, sonny boy. Get me the box. And hurry."

"Mom!" Gary screamed as he saw his mother driving away with the box in the backseat of the car. He ran all the way to his gramps's house and told him about it.

"I thought she knew about it and wouldn't let on. Come on, we have to prepare for the hell that's coming our way."

Gramps covered all the windows and cracks with newspaper to prevent light from coming through. He explained as best he could while doing all this.

"Now let me see if I can give you the short version of this sordid event that took place a few years ago. We were playing in the woods, my brothers and I, along with some friends, twelve of us, if I remember correctly, when there came a sudden flash of light that wasn't lightning, and a sudden roar in the heavens that wasn't thunder. We all scampered for safety, but in the forest, there's lots of places to run but not to hide. Every secret place was well lit. I was the coward, so I chose a tree and decided to sit there with my head in my arms, crying like a girl. After what seemed like hours but was probably a few minutes, all was quiet and the bright lights were gone, along with my brothers and friends. I tried to stand and found I couldn't. I was stuck to something."

"The box?"

"You guessed right. There were symbols drawn on the cover of it when I finally got loose."

"I know the rest of the story."

Gramps spun around to face Gary, who was standing ten feet tall, with a beard and the largest bodily frame one could imagine. With a silly grin on his face, he said, "We're free, Gramps."

"That's insulting. How dare you call me Gramps? Gary! Snap your thumb and middle finger. Now."

Gary did and he was back to normal. He sat down heavily as though he was drained of all energy. He wiped away the sweat that was forming on his brow.

"Do you know the rest of the story?" Gramps asked him.

"Yes. I'm completely aware of everything whenever they shadow me since drinking the concoction. So the twelve brothers in the box are your childhood friends and your biological brothers?" Gary wanted to know.

"Used to be. Not so anymore. I don't know how they got in there or from where the box came. I do know that they've been trouble ever since. But they're more trouble if I don't use them."

"Sounds kind of complicated if they value their freedom so much."

"Their freedom lies in their captivity and being told what to do and when to do it."

"Where does Mom fit into all this?"

"She found the box when she was little and when one of the brothers was ready to go back home, as it were. He was all spent from cutting and slashing all day. Know about all the unsolved murders too horrendous to describe throughout the years? And then suddenly some poor soul is captured and branded a serial killer? That would be one of them."

"So if I don't get cleared, I'll be a serial killer?"

"I think your mother is working on something now to prevent that."

"Then she'd better hurry."

Gary again passed out, and this time he was a fully developed handsome monster able to disappear and reappear at will.

Gary went out on the town, followed by his grandfather, who was unable to do anything anymore. In reality, Gramps was pulled along against his will and compelled to watch the destruction and mayhem perpetrated by his grandson on all with whom he came into contact.

The knife remained in his hand while he cut and slashed his way along with a smile on his face.

In the middle of town, they heard the shout, "Dad! Gary!" There was Gary's mother with the opened box in her hand and fury on her face.

"Dad! You didn't explain the dangers of leaving the box open? Gary? I love you, my son, but this has to end here and now." And she threw a liquid in his face, which made him laugh in her face. She was dumbstruck because it was supposed to kill him. It had the opposite effect.

"No, Mother dearest. Your son, Gary, is dead. We are here now. What's the name of the many from your good book? Oh yes, it is Legion, for we are many. And I like this town. Plenty to do here." And he twisted her neck. "Together we shall even the population."

Gramps tried to run but couldn't.

"No, Gramps, you shall be my witness. After all, how often has it been said that the world is overpopulated."

THE RUNNING SHOES

I was so looking forward to Grandma's wake that I couldn't eat for a week. Her death was predicted to happen at four o'clock in the afternoon of the Friday following the annual harvest.

It would be my first. Hearing about it from family members throughout the years, I expected it to be an exciting affair. I turned sixteen the month before, so I'm eligible to attend a wake. My clothes were all ready, including shoes. I did ask, "Why running shoes?" but got no answer. I didn't remember any of them using running shoes to attend a wake. But then I suppose they did not reveal all that happened at that time.

Grandma did go to sleep on the date and time predicted. I was dressed and ready a full three hours early. I was so eager to be among the grown-ups. There were a lot of speculations about the topics for discussion. I wondered aloud whether it would be a business meeting.

As we approached the house of mourning, the drums and singing were so loud, it was enough to wake the dead. I walked into the living room, and there, sitting around the dining table, were the children and brothers and sisters of Grandma. All twenty-six of them. At a smaller table were the grandchildren who were of age, talking and laughing.

Then the men, dressed in what appeared to be loincloths and headbands, started the bongo drums. Then the dancers came in, swirling and shaking their waistline and stamping their feet. Meanwhile the candles that were lighting all around the room were blazing like so many flambeaux.

When they asked me to sing the hymn that would herald the waking of Grandma, I was mortified.

"What? What do you mean the waking of Grandma?" I asked with the accompanying amount of sixteen-year-old impertinence.

"This is her wake, honey. And since you're the newest, you'll have to do the honors."

Since I couldn't get out of it and the only exit was blocked by the aging family members, I started the hymn. When I got to the second verse, I followed the eyes of all and saw Grandma sitting up in her coffin, arms outstretched and holding out a pot of gold.

I dropped the hymnal and made a beeline for the exit, jumping over tables and chairs, and I don't know, but I'm sure I knocked down a few of the older people.

I now know the purpose of the running shoes.

REVENGE GONE WRONG

The circumstances and events surrounding the death of Mr. John McAdams are wide and varied. So too are the thoughts and comments on everything relating to the incidents involved. Though young Delaney was arrested for the crime, he did a grand job of defending himself and got away on a technicality. He was not guilty, of course. He was just in the wrong place at the wrong time. But he was still ostracized by all, including his family. Even with no proof, they were all sure of his guilt.

He lost his job, his landlady evicted him with two days' notice, and he lived on the streets for about two months. With all these obstacles, he still managed to keep his head up. He took it all in stride. Eventually he opened a bookstore, and in a matter of a few short years, he met and married a beautiful girl from a neighboring county, had two children, a son and a daughter, a grand house at the end of the main street, and was living well. His store was turning a huge profit because it was the only bookstore for miles around. Plus, he regularly had authors in store for book signings and talks. That was a treat for the children of the community because it was something one would see only on television. So the parents had no choice but to give their children permission to attend such events. They would have cut classes to visit the store anyway, thereby causing so much more trouble for them.

Delaney used to be called 'dhal belly' from age 5 because of his penchant for eating dhal every day, and he had a paunch that never left him. He was a jolly fellow and always joking around. He used to make everybody laugh with his antics. But as he grew older and his love for reading and acquiring knowledge increased, he became dull, and everyone picked on him, though most times it went unnoticed. He was always engaged in matters too complex for their understanding.

After a particularly unhappy year at school, he left to pursue other interests, returning only to visit his family. The taunts continued well into his manhood, casting aspersions on his masculinity, but it didn't appear to be hurting him. He handled it all pretty well.

It was around this period that Mr. John McAdams was found dead in the ravine behind the primary school, his throat slit from ear to ear and a long gash from shoulder to belly button. It was a habit of Delaney to sit atop the plum tree near this same ravine and read one of his many books, with only the birds as companions. He always brought along scraps of food for them. The body was found a few hours after Delaney had left for his home. The people said he drank the blood and ate the liver and heart raw, so he'd be intelligent and understand as well as remember everything he read.

One fine and sunny day, he was out with his family frolicking in the park. His wife had made a picnic basket with all their favorite snacks, and she even included the music box playing all their favorite calypsos and soca. They were all having fun when suddenly the rains came pouring down. The weatherman had said no rain for the next two days.

Delaney watched, incredulous, as the rain messed up his wife's hair. It got all stringy, and she looked like a wet fowl. He knew how much time and money went into that special hairdo for this day, which he didn't mind at all. He loved his wife very much and would go to any length to keep that smile on her face. There was also a bit of gratitude and appreciation for her not turning her back on him in the face of all the adversities and obstacles that came his way in the form of sneers and snickers.

The picnic was ruined. He was stiff with anger and held his fists so tightly closed that his fingernails cut deep into his flesh and he bled profusely, though he didn't appear to notice.

Crying long tears at the disastrous outcome of the long-awaited outing, Lucinda packed up the soggy remains of food and snacks and bundled everything, including children, into the car. She called out to her husband, and only then did she notice the rigidity of his stance. She called him again, this time touching his arm. He exploded with such a string of obscenities, words that you'd hear only from the riffraff of society or from the construction workers on payday, that she was speechless.

Delaney watched as Lucinda ran to the car and drove away at breakneck speed. He was devastated in that his wife was now afraid of him. She has joined all his enemies in ostracizing him through no fault of his own. He could see that she hated and resented him under the pretext of being afraid. He didn't cause the rain to fall, did he? It was the fault of the weatherman. He'd predicted no rain. Delaney swore that he'd get him for causing his wife to resent him.

With gnashing teeth and a perfect screw face, Delaney walked the two miles to his home, stopping briefly at the hardware to collect some much-needed supplies. Rain was pouring bucket a drop, but he appeared unaffected by it all. He was soaking wet and looked like a frizzle fowl when he tried the door to his house and found it locked.

He banged and banged frantically, to no avail. The door just would not open. He stamped the ground and shook his fists at the heavens to show how furious he was, specifically at the weatherman for his blatant lie in saying no rain and spoiling everything for him. He hurled expletives and stones and whatever he could get his hands on at passersby. They ran when they saw the supplies from the hardware and guessed at his intentions.

Delaney retrieved a hidden key from the back shed that was almost forgotten since it's was put there when they first moved in. Just in case, he said. Never said in case of what, though. He let himself in with the supplies from the hardware. He collected his bearings and went into the kitchen and prepared a meal for his family. He loved cooking, his favorite being pelau with either a coleslaw or something green like patchoi or cauliflower with white sauce. His family always enjoyed his cooking. All the while singing a calypso and dancing along to the music from his own head. Delaney then showered, dressed, and quite nicely called his family to eat.

They were at the table when the doorbell rang. Lucinda made a move to get up when Delaney said too softly, "Don't." So she didn't. She continued with her dinner while the knocking continued unabatedly. She realized how on edge was her husband, and she secretly prayed for the visitor to leave.

"Are you praying, honey?" asked Delaney, and she involuntarily jumped, so startled was she. She didn't realize that she was praying aloud.

"Well, I um, um…" she stammered.

"You don't have to, dear. Everything's fine," he said.

As the knocking continued. Delaney went to answer the door. When he came back, he explained there was some problem with the neighbors but it was rectified. They finished their dinner with no more interruptions and went to bed with a night full of uncertainties. Needless to say, Lucinda did not sleep.

Things were fine over the next week, but Delaney got home whistling a particular tune every day, and it was so monotonous as to be annoying to the entire household.

"Mr. John McAdams is playing the fool with me. He knows who killed him, yet he wouldn't say," Delaney muttered and grumbled while sharpening an already sharp cutlass on the sharpening stone in the shed. "He let the authorities railroad me into jail for two months while he happily and joyfully and gleefully tromped about the village, watching me squirm. He looked on while my parents and sisters and brothers ostracized me. No, he was not a nice man. And now he is in cahoots with the weatherman to spoil everything for me and my family. They won't get away with it. No, they won't."

He was rambling on within the shed, with the tools and figments of his imagination that was slowly taking form, as his only companions. He stopped momentarily when he heard a faint sound from without. He rushed to open the door and saw his wife weeding the grass around her flower plants using a foot-long cutlass that he'd fashioned for her to make her gardening easier. He watched her with his screw face and quietly closed the door.

Lucinda listened to his grumblings under the pretext of gardening and didn't allow that she saw him looking at her. She had to know how and when to protect and defend their children. Delaney had always been a good husband and father, and she'd hate to have to abandon him now in his hour of need. But not at the expense of their safety. She gathered the weeds in a bundle and was taking it to the compost heap when she noticed a plot of ground freshly dug and refilled. Thinking that she had some time, she investigated and saw shoes just about a few inches under. With presence of mind, she hastily covered it up and went back to the house and started packing a few clothes in preparation for nightfall when she could sneak out.

Meanwhile, back in the shed, Delaney discovered a hidden trap door that he was unaware existed. The house and outbuildings were bought from a very old man who never did interact with anyone, and they never bothered to really investigate all the property. They didn't need it, they said, because they weren't going to be doing any large-scale gardening. However, at this juncture, the time seemed appropriate for seeking out the ins and outs of this trap door.

He went down the narrow ladder and was surprised at the long corridor facing him. He explored and found what appeared to be a kitchen with a kerosene stove and lots of glass jars containing all sorts of uncanny stuff, like roots and eyes and beans, rat tails, and unrecognizable nameless things. He remembered the stories he heard as a child about the first peoples to inhabit this land, the last of whom was the old man, and believed it was all old wives' tales. But here in front of him was proof of the power they claimed to have been possessed by these indigenous people. If only he knew how to use these ingredients, he'd give all the conspirators a run for their money, starting with the weatherman. This way, no police would be involved.

Then he spied a dusty old book on a bottom shelf. After dusting it, he read the title, which must have been written about a hundred years ago. He could make out just one word, *Recipes*. He was so disappointed, he threw the book across to the other end of the corridor and continued rummaging. He espied more books, all titled *Recipes*. He opened one of them with a loud steups, and much to his surprise, he found that it contained recipes of spells and incantations, along with seals for different requests and whatever your heart desires.

He found a crude but legible map of the entire area with directions to rooms and the different ingredients. Also an altar for burning candles and incense. Delaney was so elated he could feel the tension in his body being replaced with happy feelings, and he didn't like it. He would become susceptible to the taunts of others again, and he didn't want that. The angry feeling gave him a sense of power. He had the guts to do anything, mash up the place or stone down the people who cross him. He jumped for joy when he read a recipe that would have him in a constant state of vexation. He tried the formula and found that it really worked. He could feel the muscles in his face tightening, and no smile would emerge when he tried.

He stayed away from the main house 'cause he really didn't want to hurt his family. They must be safe. They are not responsible for what these other people were doing. He called up the secretary at his bookstore and informed her that he wouldn't be in for a few days. He explored the various rooms that was underground and deliberately searched for the altar. He mentally planned and plotted who was going first and what he'd do with them using the recipe book.

He spent the entire night researching and ensuring that he got the correct names for the appropriate bottles. The language was difficult to understand in that what he knew as St. John's bush, which when boiled would turn the water blood red, in this book, was called cockroach grass. And what he knew as vervain was called venven. And various other anomalies. He searched and researched and wracked his brain, trying to recall the stories he'd heard from his childhood up. He desperately needed those stories and their meanings now more than ever.

He traversed the corridors of the underground facility, for want of a better word, throughout the night. Then he hit the nail on the head when he fell asleep on the cold hard floor and dreamt the answers to his unvoiced questions. He came to the realization that he is a direct descendant of said indigenous folk and had the power. Maybe that is why he handled all the bullying from such a tender age so coldly and just about snapped in adulthood. It was time to fight back.

He got together the paraphernalia needed for invoking the dead and went to the graveyard to call up John McAdams. That done, he sent him on his way to the weatherman to wreak havoc in his life but not kill him. The weatherman must be made to suffer untold miseries.

Three days later, Delaney showed up at the bookstore and began shouting at his secretary.

"What is this?" he screamed at her. "There is dust everywhere. What do I pay you for? To prim yourself in the bathroom all day? Oh yes. You think I don't know?" Delaney was all red in the face, and a vein seemed to be swelling in his forehead.

"But, Mr. Delaney—" Stephanie began, but he stopped her.

"Don't 'Mr. Delaney' me! Get to work and clean up this place. Where are the proceeds of the days' sales?"

"No sales today!" she shouted at him. "It's been only five minutes since the store opened!"

She glared at him while he glared right back. "Whatever is your problem, deal with it yourself. I have my problems. You don't see me bringing them to you," she finished on the verge of tears.

Delaney softened a bit and touched her on the shoulder, saying soothingly, "I'm sorry. I thought only I had problems. Literally. Take the day off. Come back tomorrow."

"Thank you. My brother was found in the bathroom this morning covered in blood. Apparently he'd spent half the night in there slicing himself with a knife," she said through heartbreaking sobs.

"You have a brother? How old is he? Will he be all right?"

"I guess. The hospital assigned a psychiatrist to evaluate him. He is only twenty-four. A brilliant meteorologist. Such a bright future ahead of him. My mother is devastated." She blew her nose into the handkerchief that was handed to her and didn't see the wicked grin on Delaney's face.

"You mean the weatherman on channel WXPO?"

She nodded and burst into more sobbing.

Delaney, though in a perpetual state of vexation, managed to smile through it all while asking the driver to take her home or wherever she wanted to go.

Delaney closed the shop and went back home, choosing side streets and alleyways to be away from people. He was ecstatic that the two spells had worked beautifully. When he placed the commands to John McAdams, he was skeptical as to the results. He did follow the recipe, but the commands was where he encountered some problems. He had to be precise in his wordings, so he improvised, and the results was astounding. The weatherman sliced himself but did not die. He will, however, be suffering for the rest of his life, being referred to as a madman. No way will he ever get another job. And his parents will soon tire of him, just like his own parents had. Now all and sundry will be paid for all that was done to him, from calling him 'dhal belly' and culminating in his wife being afraid of him and leaving with their children.

He slammed his fist on the steering wheel so hard that it bent. Apparently the vexation spell had some unexpected side effects. His strength has been steadily increasing.

He didn't realize he was speeding, and he almost drove into the wide-open ditch where the workmen neglected to put up a caution sign. He stepped on the brakes and came to a screeching halt. He got out of the car and looking left and right, saw when some of the neighbors quickly turned back to what they were doing, pretending they didn't see a thing. He knew there'd be no witnesses, as usual, but no matter, he now had the means to fix them all good and proper. He let out a string of expletives in their direction and jumped in his car and sped away.

Delaney went straight to work on the spells that would hurt them all, the entire community if he had the time.

He collected the ingredients from the shelves, donned the special black coat with red sash along with the skull cap that he believed was the accepted garb for performing the ritual, and headed for the altar. He must first ask permission to use the stuff and get guidance and the power so that it would all go according to his wishes. He lit the candles that were already in place and got down to the nitty-gritty part of it.

Absolutely sure he had the power and wherewithal to create maximum havoc to all, he decided to add another ingredient to enhance the result. He left home on foot, so as to better able to throw the coins into the yards of each and every house along the main road. Contained in a pouch tied around his waist, it made for easy access to take, and with a swing of the arm, he threw them into the yards, with no one being the wiser. It would appear that he was exercising while walking.

He woke bright and early next morning and switched on the television for news. He expected the results to come in fast and furious because of the added ingredient.

First to be reported was the sighting of Mr. John McAdams in the vicinity of the weatherman's house. The entire community was of a very superstitious nature, so it wasn't too long before the news spread, and there were prayers and the lighting of candles and a few people trying their hand at being exorcists. They were sure that it was the ghost of the murdered man that caused the incident with the weatherman. However, that was short lived because there was another incident, whereby another family got into a heated argument and several of the members were severely chopped. The ambulance was kept busy the entire night.

Delaney used some more of the vexation spell and went driving out to inspect his work.

He came across a group of individuals all disheveled and worried, discussing the happenings, and since they were all agitated, he went up to them to add salt to the wounds.

"Hello, everyone, there seem to be something troublesome going on. What is it?" he inquired with concern.

"Troublesome? It's horrendous! There's been chopping and stealing, attempted suicides, and everything horrible. Someone even said the ghost of John McAdams has been roaming the entire area for the past week!"

"You're joking, right? A ghost? Do people still believe in such things?"

"Of course, there are ghosts. They haunt and terrorize people for no apparent reason."

"You should know that, Delaney. Wasn't it your grand uncle who was the official exorcist?"

"Yes. I believe he was."

"Well? Isn't it possible that he left some door or something open for the ghosts to come through?"

"And John McAdams did die with a lot of blood seeping from him."

"It is said that however the person dies, that's how they affect those they choose to haunt. And his killer was set free."

"You are responsible for all of this, Delaney."

It shouldn't have surprised him, but it did. They just ganged up on him for showing a bit of concern. *That does it*, he said to himself. Aloud, he told them, "I'm glad you are all in a living hell now. May this day and this night go on and on till the third and fourth generation. And may you live to see your generations get paid for the words you utter on this day." He appeared so calm when he uttered that curse that they were speechless, envisioning all sorts of harm and unfortunate accidents happening to their descendants. Delaney knew the effect his words would have on them.

He walked away with heavy footsteps, going a little further down the street, surveying his handiwork. He could find no pleasure in it anymore. He was satisfied, but not happy. There was a stoop to his shoulders, and with hands in pocket, head lowered, he gazed on the houses darkened because of a power cut. Men and boys in drunken stupor were flinging bottles at anything that moved. Even the priest came out in his underwear, using the most foul language. There was no joy in the result of his work. Delaney turned around and trudged his way back to his home.

On his way to the kitchen, he passed in front of a mirror and saw a reflection of himself. He stopped and backtracked. No, it couldn't be. Now he actually looked at the reflection. He'd aged about twenty years. How could that be? What did he do wrong?

He raced to the shed and made a beeline for the recipe book. After reading it, he was satisfied that he'd followed it all to the letter. So why did he age so? He traversed the corridor, scratching his head, mentally searching for the answer.

"Honey?"

He spun as if on wheels. "What are you doing here?" he asked his wife, his words gruff to his own ears.

"What have you done, sweetheart?" she asked gently, walking up to him with one hand at her back.

"I've had enough. I couldn't take it anymore." He broke down in tears. "When I saw your hair. The rain. He said no rain. John

111

McAdams was a bad man. He refused to tell them that I didn't kill him. And he knew who did it."

"He was already dead when they found him, honey. He couldn't tell them anything." Lucinda tried to reach him, even though she knew he was gone mentally.

"So what if he was dead? The dead have power, don't you know that? Of course you do."

"You're not making any sense, Delaney."

"You called me Delaney. You never call me Delaney. You're not my wife."

Delaney straightened up with a jerk. Gone were the tears, and in its place was a man with the most gruesome expression. His brows furrowed and lips thin, he sauntered toward her, raising his fist to strike when she suddenly presented to him a pouch in the palm of her hand. He stopped dead in his tracks and stared at it.

"Where did you get that?" he asked her with a drawl that was so unrecognizable to him, that he scratched his throat and repeated the question, but it was more pronounced.

"Right where you left it. You used the compelling liquid, Delaney. You applied it to your face, didn't you? This is danger-ous stuff. Have you looked at yourself? You are metamorphosing, Delaney, into something terrifying."

"What do you mean? I feel fine."

"No, you don't. We were doing so well. People always talk. So what? We were still happy."

"I couldn't bear anymore, Lucinda. I had to put a stop to it."

"No, Delaney, What you did was inexcusable and unforgivable. I have to stop it for the sake of the children."

"What do you mean?"

"This place belonged to my ancestors. I knew all about it. I never expected you to come down here and use this stuff."

"What are you going to do?"

"Well, I can't possibly destroy my heritage so...."

Lucinda waved her hand in the air, and Delaney disintegrated.

THE EVIL MERMAID

Mad as hell, Claudine watched the puddle of water forming in the middle of the kitchen and steups loud and long enough to precipitate a visit to the dentist. She recognized it as a sign of impending doom.

Vincent, Claudine's husband for going on ten years, didn't return with the group of fishermen at the appointed time, so she went looking for him at Saut d'Eau beach.

The unusually harsh sound of the waves rolling onto the stones was grating the nerves so much that it would send the feeble ones running home. But not Claudine. She was on a mission, an impossible one albeit, but accomplish said mission she would. Or all hell would break loose on this sleepy fishing village tonight.

"Are you sure the last time you saw Vincent he was going into the ajoupa?" she asked Martin again.

"Yes. He just went in and vanished," Martin reiterated.

"A mermaid got him."

"Are you loco, Claudine? Mermaids don't take people."

"They take men. And I'm going to get back my husband in a few days or my name is not Claudine the Amazon. Yes, I know your nickname for me."

Martin gazed at her forehead, the all too familiar vein swelling, signaling trouble on the horizon.

"Sorry," Martin whispered under his breath. "Want help?"

"No thanks. I can handle it," she replied.

That night, Claudine positioned herself where she could see the mermaids when they come out to comb their hair. They love to sit on that special rock and sing their haunting melodies.

They were taken aback by the sudden appearance of Claudine, who rose up from behind another rock, causing them to dash back into the water, one of them forgetting her comb, which is what Claudine hoped for. She took the comb home and waited.

At midnight, she heard the mournful cry, and out came Claudine, with the rifle specially equipped with a sixpence piece. She was nude, with her hair tied in one ponytail with a red ribbon.

"Why are you bothering me at this unholy hour?" she asked the mermaid, who was cowering in the underbrush.

"I've come for my comb," answered the mermaid.

"What do I get in return?"

"It is my comb. You cannot sell it to me."

Claudine knew that while the comb was in her possession, she could ask anything and the mermaid would have to honor her request.

"I found it. Finders keepers. Go back where you come from."

"I must have my comb. Please."

"Okay. This is what I want. One of you stole my husband. Which one and where do I find her? Tell me and you get your comb."

"Okay, I'll show you. Grab my hair."

She immediately swung her long golden hair, which wrapped itself around Claudine's hands when she made contact.

"Now close your eyes and watch."

Claudine later armed herself with a silver knife prepared for this purpose and headed to the cave beneath the sea to extract her husband from the jaws of the evil mermaid. The entrance was guarded by a dozen or so mermaids. Inside the cave was no water, well-lighted and tastefully decorated with the most exotic sweet-smelling flowers. She sliced through the wall of mermaids, holding her breath from the deadly fragrance, still wearing the red ribbon that acted as a spiritual guard against all unworldly forces. Their scales fell off quite easily with a swipe of the knife and she got to Vincent, who was enjoying a meal of yellow rice.

"Come, Vincent, let's go home." She reached for him, but he pulled back and asked who was she. Shocked beyond belief, Claudine slapped him hard across the face to bring him to his senses, but to no avail. Hearing laughter in the background, she understood that being under the spell from the one who kidnapped him, he couldn't think clearly.

She got hold of one of the mermaids and asked her, "What's wrong with him? What have you all done to my husband?"

"We didn't do anything. We are just the security. It was Marshimha. She said she finally met the man she wants and is going to make him her very own."

"Not if I have anything to say about it. He is mine."

Claudine raised the knife to slice off the head of the mermaid, but she said that she could counteract the spell.

"How?" Claudine asked eagerly.

The mermaid then hastily gave her step-by-step instructions on how to combat Marshimha's spell.

"I understand. Where is Marshimha?"

"Behind you."

Claudine spun, holding the knife at her waist, and sliced open Marshimha's stomach. She coldly and deftly removed the liver and gouged out her eyes. Claudine fried the liver and scrambled the eyes, like the security said, and ate it all. Infused now with the power of the mermaids, she went and collected her husband, who was now free from all spells.

"Vincent, I'm so happy to have you back home with me."

"Claudine, if that is your name, get out of my house. Now. I don't have a wife!" His tone was so filled with cold hatred, that Claudine back stepped and held on to the kitchen counter to steady herself.

She went back to the cave, but it was no longer there.

Resurfacing, her feet got caught in some seaweed, then she heard the voice of the security telling her where to go because Marshimha was still alive. Freed from the weed, she set out to the rock, where she found Marshimha lying prone with a wicked smile on her now grotesque face.

"Vincent will never be yours. He is mine." Her voice was strong and hard. Claudine removed the red ribbon and tied it at the end of Marshimha's tail.

"What are you doing?" she asked feebly, a sign that the red ribbon was working.

Marshimha vanished in a cloud of dust.

"Claudine? Where are you?" Vincent was calling her name, and smiling, she ran to meet him.

She didn't see the other mermaids dancing their thanks to her for freeing them from the evil mermaid.

JAKE AND THE ZOMBIES

Jeanette clutched the file in her hands with a smile spread across her face from ear to ear. She was happy the deal was completed. She hurried home to her husband, Larry, and their three children: Madonna, Chuck, and Jake. There were squeals of laughter in the old house on this particular day.

"Is this for real, Mom? We got our own house?" asked Chuck, who'd been listening to his parents talk about having their own house for so long that it was now to him like a mantra.

"Yes, dodo head. There are the papers. So we celebrate with what?" asked Madonna, who will use any reason for a celebration. She was a happy-go-lucky eighteen-year-old of a tomboy. She kept her hair cut very short indeed and refused to grow it, for fear she'd look girly. Yecch! Not acceptable. Jake sat in his corner of the couch as usual, not taking part in anything. As far as he's concerned, they are all too loud and rambunctious. They have no discipline. He was sure a mistake had been made at the hospital on the day of his birth. This cannot be his biological family.

But he was remembering the little chat he'd overheard. His father was terminally ill. There is no cure. He's got some kind of disease as yet unnamed. Jake walked away from them and the entire household to be alone with his morbid thoughts. Being the middle child is not all it's cracked up to be. He found himself in the middle of the forest, and not knowing which way to turn, he sat at the foot of a tree and went to sleep. He woke to see three men in large hats and black overcoats whispering.

A clandestine operation, he thought to himself. He remained still so as not to announce his presence. They lifted a trap door camouflaged with grass and were swallowed up by the earth. He waited a few minutes and was about to sneak after them when he heard a voice.

"What you doing?"

The voice shocked him, and he turned around to see a girl about his age with short curly hair behind him.

"Shh," he whispered. They went down the ladder into a dirty old room with a table, one chair, and a light that soon extinguished itself.

"I'm afraid of the dark," said the girl.

"So go back."

"And let you have all the fun? No way."

They followed the muffled sound of voices till it was loud enough to understand.

"Yes, gentlemen. With the contents of this little vial, we can live our entire lives free from pain and sickness until our natural death."

"What did you say it's called?"

"It's called the breath of life. But we have enough for only one hundred people."

"Why so?"

"The person who came up with this formula has since died. And there is no one with the expertise to replicate it. His notes, along with the formula, can't be found. We'll be auctioning some at a location soon to be announced. You gentlemen have the honor of deciding who shall receive the breath of life." The men soon left, leaving the vial in a glass dish on the wooden table.

Jake emptied the contents of the vial into the coffeepot and left on his bike.

His father, who overslept, rushed out without drinking his coffee.

His mother, who couldn't bear to see anything wasted, screwed her face and drank it all. Then she had her cup of tea to counteract the awful taste of coffee.

Jake paid no attention to the sirens, which was a daily occurrence in this part of the city where he worked doing odd jobs for the owner of the local supermarket. However, when the customers and workers ran out in droves, he followed.

The crowd stopped where the East Dry River met the sea. Pushing through the crowd to get a better view of what was happening, he was disgusted to see a woman on all fours, head bowed like an animal, eating something that was all bloody. On closer inspection, he recognized his mother's clothing.

It couldn't be.

But it was.

That was what she was wearing when he left home not too long ago. What could have happened in that short space of time?

He looked at the police just standing around, with their guns trained on her, a frown etched on their faces and the crowd shocked into silence. The woman turned around with a jerk, maybe because of a strange sound or scent, couldn't tell which, but dropping her food, she sprinted and leaped out of the Dry River, which was walled on both sides to keep the water from flooding the city in the rainy season. That spurred the cops into action, and they let out a volley of shots but didn't hit the woman, who was out of sight in a few seconds.

Jake ran to his home a few blocks away while calling his father on his cell phone.

"Dad? How was Mom when you left this morning?" he asked as soon as he got an answer.

"She was fine. Left her sleeping. I was late and rushed out without my coffee. Is something wrong?" The concern in his father's voice was nothing new.

"There's some kind of commotion down by the Dry River. Some woman eating dogs."

Jake recognized the voice as that of the apprentice.

"Must be pipers spreading rumors to get people out of their homes so they could go in and steal," Jake heard his father say. "I'll call you back, Jake."

"Johnny, what's going on?"

"Mr. McKay, they caught some crazy old woman eating a dog down in the Dry River."

"Nonsense. Get back to work," he ordered them.

Jake rushed into the house and went straight to the coffeepot. Empty. His father did not drink it. Did his mother? But she never drank coffee. She hates the stuff. His mind in a whirl, he wondered about the ingredients in that vial. He tried to recollect the conversation he'd overheard. They did say it was a cure-all. He rushed out to find the girl who was with him when he made the discovery, only to realize he had no idea where to find her. He went to the spot where he'd heard the conversation, but not too close, and scratching his head tried to decipher the meaning of it all. A slight sound caused him to slowly turn around. There he saw what made him empty his bowels in shock. It was the girl, but she was not the same. Her hair was now stringy and black where it had been curly and light brown. He clutched his stomach, grimacing and transfixed at the growl and stench emanating from her. He didn't notice a person with a shotgun behind him.

"Don't move an inch." He recognized the voice as that of the man offering the breath of life for sale. The breath of life. No more diseases or sickness. No pain. No Alzheimer's. And whatever your complaint, now it's cured. Never to return.

Not daring to breathe, he raised his eyebrow, and the man pointed at the girl with his chin. Jake focused his attention on her as she stood upright, but her knees were all twisted and her feet turned backward. The man whispered, "Run!" and Jake took off like the wind. He'd had no idea he could run that fast. The man let go a volley of shots, then ran after Jake, who turned just in time to see the girl sprinting like she was at the Olympics. Unable to think clearly, he made a beeline for his home, where he met with what he believed to be his mother, holding his father in a viselike grip, head thrown back, mouth open revealing some canine teeth, twisted and greenish. His father, not able to move a muscle or comprehend what was happening to his wife, squeezed his eyes shut.

The man shot at his mother and blew a hole right through her midsection without harming his father, who fell on his back and stayed put. His mother bared her teeth and came after them. The man again shot her, but it didn't stop her from coming fast.

Finding his voice at last, Jake shouted, "What happened to her?" They both dashed into the house and locked the door.

"The breath of life happened to her," he stated as a matter of fact.

"What?" Jake exclaimed, looking at him, confused.

"You stole the breath of life and gave it to her, am I right?" A slight movement caused the man to raise his gun, and Jake shouted, "No! That's my brother and sister."

They both were cowering in a corner, fearing the worst.

"Jake? What's going on?" Madonna's voice trembled uncontrollably.

"Well, I…uh…" Jake stymied for an answer.

"You gave her the entire vial. And she was healthy." The man looked at him knowingly.

"I didn't mean to. I put it in the coffeepot for my father. He's dying."

"Even so, young man, only one drop is necessary. As it is, giving all of it to a healthy person kills them for half an hour and then they're alive again. They become what you see in front of you now."

"So how do we get rid of it? She's no longer my mother."

"I don't know. But what happened to the girl? Did she drink it too?"

"She probably experimented."

"You thieves. I really should leave you in your mess. But I can't. When the authorities find out, there'll be hell to pay."

"Why? It's just a simple mistake."

"This here is what you call unapproved research. This sort of thing was designed to cure, but some of the side effects was changing tastes and desires, enhancing strength, and acquiring different perceptions."

"So the gist of it is, she's not going to die. She'll go on forever and ever."

"That's a very long time. We'll be dead by then."

"What if she scratches us or something?"

The man bowed his head, shaking it vigorously. "Don't think about that."

Jake, cupping an ear with his hand, said, "Listen."

"It's quiet."

"Exactly. What's she doing? Where's Dad?" Jake searched until he found his father on the kitchen floor, disoriented. He was pale and feverish. He got an ice pack, placed it on his forehead, and asked Madonna and Chuck to watch over him.

"Don't worry, the house is burglar proof, with some good-quality wrought iron. The zombies can't get in."

"You label Mom a zombie, Jake?"

"Fight me later. Stay here." Jake went to find the man looking intently across to the woods surrounding the house.

"There's more of them?" Jake, shocked at the numbers, almost screamed. "How did that happen?"

"I've no idea. But we have to get out of here." Stating the obvious, the man moved around like a headless chicken.

"How? They're quite fast. What is your name?" Jake asked him.

"Dr. Michelin. Maybe they'll slow down with time."

"What was that?"

"Came from the kitchen."

They both turned to face the kitchen, and there in the doorway was his father and two sisters. All three had grown in mass, hair got stringy, eyes red, and what appeared to be deep gashes lining their cheeks. The stench from them overpowering.

They were leaning over to take up their shirts to cover their noses when they were grabbed by the scruff of their necks.

LEAH, THE CURSED ONE

I positioned myself at the back of the sports bar enjoying a whiskey and soda amid the din of the weekend crowd. Dark as it was in this little corner, I was still noticed by the old man with the grizzly beard and long aquiline nose. He shuffled across to me bearing two drinks and offered me one while he pulled out a chair and made himself comfortable. I let loose a long audible sigh that would ordinarily chase away the most gullible but not this one.

"I see I'm just in time."

"You are? What for, may I ask?"

"Well, it's a long weekend, and a young beautiful girl drinking all alone in a place like this, there must be a problem."

I didn't want to talk but couldn't help myself. "Let's see now, according to your calculation, long weekend, young and beautiful, plus drinking alone equals problem?"

"Sounds silly when you put it like that, but yes. You do have a problem."

"And do you know the nature of this problem?"

"Actually I do. You so despise your mother that you're sure she's stupid and refuse to heed her guidance. All that she taught you from childhood, you've thrown out with the trash. Including words and action for your well-being, hence your predicament at this time."

"Look, mister, you're crossing the line. I do have respect for your age, but that's about it."

"Quiet. Let me finish. You've recently moved into an apartment where some grisly murders were committed."

"Okay, you've got my attention."

"Your mother comes from a long line of seers. But they all had one thing missing. They couldn't do anything about what they saw."

"Tell me something I don't know."

"You were all disobedient, impudent, no-good bitches as children right up to your twenties. And you all die horribly." He studied my face till he was satisfied he'd gotten a reaction.

"I repeat tell me something I don't know."

"You're going to have a great time at your party tonight. An eye opener, you might say," he stated matter-of-factly.

"That's enough." I left then with a big fat steps.

Just out the door, I met the girls coming in. "Hi. In there is dead. Go elsewhere."

"We're only making up time to get to your place later."

"My place? What do you mean?" But I got no answer. They were giggling so much they didn't hear me. Knowing I had nothing planned for my place, I shrugged and went on.

"Are you following me?" I asked the old man when I noticed he was walking in the same direction as I.

"No, I'm with you," he answered matter-of-factly.

By this time, I was so angry I swung my handbag at him, but he ducked and I missed.

I turned the corner to my street, and the decorations hit me full in the face. The pumpkins were the first to catch my attention. Perfectly and professionally designed. The cobwebs with real live spiders, including a fly. As I stood there, transfixed, that voice came again.

"Beautiful, isn't it? Wait till you see the inside."

My head swiveled of its own accord and faced the old man. Feeling my eyes bulging, I couldn't utter a word. But my mouth did open. Suddenly I felt myself propelling toward my open front door. My body went from total shock and fright to total anger in an instant. The crowd inside disguised with the most horrifying masks, unlike what we're used to, the superheroes and famous serial killers from a bygone era, were having the time of their lives. Eating my food and drinking my liquor, with my music blasting away.

I don't know from where the superhuman strength came, but come it did, and I was flinging them out left right and center. But they all floated right back in and continued where they left off. My chest heaving, I faced the old man.

"What the hell is going on here? Are you responsible for this?" I screamed at him, my fists flailing like two humming birds fighting in midair.

"Me?" he asked, pointing at his face. "Oh no. You are." He smiled the wickedest smile I'd ever seen.

"Explain yourself. No riddles," I answered, still screaming.

"You didn't listen to your mother, so you ended up renting this place that has had the most grisly murders committed on this very night for two decades."

"That can't have happened. The authorities would have burnt it already."

"Only if they knew about it."

"The house or the murders?"

"Both."

"Stop looking at me. Watch what's happening." Using his chin, he pointed to the room.

The masks were all of...

I felt a chill up my spine as one made her way toward me. Though she looked familiar, I couldn't quite place her.

"Hello, Leah," she greeted me.

"Hello. I don't remember you."

"You will," she said and left sashaying.

Then there was another and another. After the fifth one greeted me by name, I asked the old man again what was happening.

"It's quite simple, really. Your family was cursed by one of your own ancestors for being disobedient."

"And the nature of that curse?"

"Should any child attain the age of fifteen and not be respectful of her mother, or be disobedient, she'll have to live in a house where no respect will be shown to her, and she'll have to eat fresh liver from a clean source once per day for eight consecutive days starting on her first Halloween, after she turns nineteen."

"I honestly don't know what to make of that story. But I do want these people out."

"Leah! I didn't know you knew so many people," Susan, a coworker, said to me.

"Phyllis! What are you doing here?"

"You can't keep me out, Leah. We go way back when." She kept moving just like the others.

"Why are you licking your lips?" the old man asked me.

"I'm not," I answered too hastily even to my ears 'cause I realized that is exactly what I was doing. I was also watching Phyllis and Susan and actually feeling the taste of that juicy liver in my mouth.

"My job here is done. Good luck," said the old man. But I was done paying attention to him.

###

ABOUT THE AUTHOR

Soter Lucio is a mother of four, grandmother of six, and great-grandmother of three. She lives alone but is never lonely because she's got the ghosts for company. They can be both friendly and spiteful, or vengeful as the case may be. But always exciting. She works as an ironer by day and writer by night.

Connect with Soter Lucio.

I really appreciate you reading my book! Here are my social media coordinates:

Friend me on Facebook: Soter Lucio

Follow me on Twitter: @JanSoter